Halley

HALLEY

A novel

FAYE GIBBONS

NewSouth Books

Montgomery

NewSouth Books
105 S. Court Street
Montgomery, AL 36104

Copyright © 2014 by Faye Gibbons
All rights reserved under International and Pan-American Copyright
Conventions. Published in the United States by NewSouth Books,
a division of NewSouth, Inc., Montgomery, Alabama.

ISBN 978-1-58838-290-0 (hardcover)
ISBN 978-1-60306-328-9 (ebook)

Library of Congress Control Number: 2014933020

Design by Randall Williams

Printed in the United States of America
by Edwards Brothers Malloy

*To my daughters-in-law, Laurie and Aca
and to my grandchildren:
Matthew, Sarah, Caleb, Isaac, Samuel, and Jacob*

Contents

1. Selling Out

HALLEY OWENBY SAT ON HER PORCH AND STUDIED THE GARDEN, the barn, the pasture, the fields, and the Georgia mountains beyond. She had seen them daily for the fourteen years of her life, but it seemed that now, when she was about to lose everything, was the first time she'd really seen them.

Her eyes dropped to the Bible on her lap. It was opened to the family register in the middle, the place marked by an old photograph of her father. Her own dark brown hair was so much like his. She had the same angular body and long legs, the same square chin and dark eyes. Grabbing up the photo, she stuck it far back in the Bible.

Her six-year-old brother, Robbie, handed her a stub of a pencil. "You going to write it?" He leaned on the arm of Halley's rocker and scratched his dog, Buck, with one bare foot.

Halley didn't want to write—didn't want to put down in black and white that her father, Jim Owenby, had died. If only refusing to write it would make it untrue! But it wouldn't. Nothing could bring him back. She straightened her shoulders. She'd always been the one in the family to face things squarely. Her father never did. Like President Roosevelt, Jim always acted as if there was no Depression or any other troubles that courage and hard work couldn't overcome.

Halley's mother was just as bad in her own way. Raised by a hellfire-and-brimstone preacher, Kate spent most of her energy trying to get a religious experience like her father preached about. Losing four babies had pushed her further in this direction. Robbie wasn't bent toward being practical, either. His head seemed always in the clouds. But he was only a little boy, Halley reminded herself.

She forced herself to focus on the first entry in the family register—her parents' marriage, fifteen years ago in 1921. The next page listed Halley's birth, followed over the next six years by three babies who had each died within days of birth. Then there was Robbie, born in 1930. One more baby came after Robbie—a boy named Will.

Finally, she came to the page headed "Deaths." Taking a deep breath, Halley hurriedly wrote her father's name below Baby Will's. "Jim Manley Owenby died July 29, 1936," she wrote, blinking back tears. Then she closed the book.

Robbie looked toward the kitchen where adult conversation hummed, and then leaned close to ask, "Is Daddy in heaven?"

"You know he is!" Halley said with more certainty than she felt. How many times she had asked herself this very question since the funeral on Wednesday! The mound of raw red dirt flashed before her and grief overtook her for several moments. She would never see her father again. Never see him attempting to tease Kate into a good mood. Never see him giving his last penny to help kinfolk or even a neighbor. Too late, she realized how much all those things meant to her. No matter what good things might happen in the future, she knew her father's death had left a gap in her life that could never be filled.

"Grandpa Franklin don't think Daddy's in heaven," Robbie whispered. "He said so to Uncle Ralph yesterday." Ralph was the oldest Franklin son. "Pa Franklin told Uncle Ralph that there was a good chance Daddy was in—in hell."

Halley was so furious she forgot caution. "How would *he* know? Pa Franklin doesn't know everything. Even if he is a preacher, *he* might be the one going to hell. The Bible says not to judge."

Robbie wrinkled his forehead. "Pa Franklin said Daddy helping Claude and Clyde with their moonshining stuff was bad as making whiskey hisself, and if Daddy hadn't been trying to help push their moonshine truck out of that ditch, then he wouldn't have been run over and . . ."

"Daddy helped people," Halley said, "and that's not bad, no matter what anybody says!"

Their Grandfather Franklin leaned out of the doorway. "You getting mighty loud out here, girl!"

He and Ma Franklin never called her or Robbie by their names, but only used "boy" or "girl." Halley often wondered what her grandparents would have done about names if the other babies had lived. "Girl one" and "girl two," maybe. "Boy three" and "boy four."

"Go nail up my Jesus sign out by the mailbox," he said. When Pa Franklin wasn't preaching, he delighted in painting signs like "Jesus saves" or "Repent!" He put them up everywhere—trees, fence posts, and abandoned buildings.

"We're out of nails," Halley answered without regret. She was tired of his frequently misspelled signs.

"Well, find some work to do." Pa Franklin expected children to be quiet and busy.

Robbie took out for the pasture with his dog, Buck. The family mules, Nip and Tuck, trotted to meet him. Robbie made pets of every animal on the farm, and he grieved over those slaughtered for food.

"Keep the boy busy," Pa Franklin told Halley, "and the both of you keep quiet. We got business to take care of in here."

And she knew what the business was. It was all her grandfather had talked about since the funeral. Halley put the Bible down on a bench and crept close to the kitchen door. Inside, the talk resumed. The insistent tone in the voices of the Franklins and the pleading note in Kate's were clear.

"Surely I can stay in my own home," Kate was saying. It sounded like a child asking permission, instead of a grown woman's statement of intention.

"Mama," Halley whispered. "You've got to stand up to them."

Ma Franklin spoke up. "People would talk, you living here all by yourself, with no man around."

"I wouldn't be alone—I'd have my children."

Ma Franklin heaved a dismissive grunt. "Young'uns don't count, and you know that well as I do. You have to think of your father. People won't think as high of a preacher with a daughter living like a loose woman."

Halley rolled her eyes. Kate? A loose woman!

Pa Franklin spoke again. "If Jim's brothers hadn't helped him out ever' time he was in a tight, *he* couldn't have worked this place. How's a *woman* going to do it? Can you plow? Can you handle mules?"

"I'm sure Claude and Clyde and their boys will help me."

Halley heard the quiver in her mother's voice.

"Yesterday after the funeral Claude mentioned giving me something on the doctor and funeral home charges," Kate went on.

Halley sucked in her breath and stepped inside. "And Uncle Clyde told me they would study how they could help."

"Girl, didn't I tell you to stay outside?" said Pa Franklin.

Halley retreated as far as the doorway and then stopped.

"What Claude and Clyde are apt to give won't be a drop in a bucket!" Pa Franklin said. "You run up all them doctor bills, and Jim died anyway. Then you just *had* to hire a funeral home to fix up the body and lay 'im out in a fancy box 'stead of letting someone right here in Alpha Springs do all that free."

"Pa, Jim always provided so generous for me and the young'uns. When he didn't have money, he traded labor for my sewing machine, Robbie's piano . . ."

"And let's don't forget the fancy screen wire, while you're at it!" said Pa Franklin. "And books to put big ideas in your daughter's head about getting an education, and a big new cook stove when the old one still worked fine. Jim Owenby knowed how to spend foolish, all right."

Ma Franklin spoke up meekly, "Well, now, the new cook stove *is* handy."

Pa Franklin glared. "Old Woman, you turning on me?"

Ma Franklin submitted at once. "No, Webb."

Kate tried again. "Gid said he could come stay a while."

Gideon was the Franklins' youngest son, and the only child left at home.

Pa Franklin exploded. "And take away the only help your poor old mama and daddy have? What are you thinking?"

Kate did not reply. They had fixed it so she could not win.

"Ever now and then you got to have cash money. You can't get out and tinker at this and that for cash like Jim done."

Halley longed to point out this admission that sometimes Jim Owenby had earned real money, but she let the moment pass and her grandfather began talking again.

"Now, you might've knowed a little about how to do things around here if Jim hadn't thought his wife was too good to dirty her hands. Jim Owenby throwed off on me that time when he come and found the Old Lady plowing. Well, I learned my wife to do ever' job I done, and now you see the reason. The way things stand, you don't know nothing about how to run this place."

Halley could bear it no longer. "I know how to work," she said. "If Ma Franklin can plow, so can I. With Claude and Clyde helping, and maybe some hired help . . ."

"Hired help!" said Pa Franklin. "My! Ain't we rich! What you going to hire *with*? And this place ain't paid off. The doctor ain't paid. The hospital ain't paid. The funeral home ain't paid. You got money hid away we don't know about?"

Kate broke into sobs.

Don't cry, Halley thought. They'll run right over you.

Sure enough, Pa Franklin smelled victory. His voice took on a businesslike tone. "I already passed the word at the funeral yesterday that you'd be selling out."

Kate raised her head. "Without talking to me?"

"No need for talk."

Well, that's that, thought Halley. Once Pa Franklin decided how things would be, no argument was allowed. The only hope was Claude or Clyde. If one of them arrived soon with sure offers of help and money, Kate might stand up to her father.

"Lum Albert said he'd buy your cows and your mules," Pa Franklin continued, "and that grown boy of his'n wants whatever of your hogs we don't take with us. Bud Gravitt says he'll buy the house and land. He must make money from that store of his. Gravitt's wife, Orrie, wants the sewing machine and the piano, if the price is right."

"Not the piano!" Halley exclaimed. "That's Robbie's. And I was hoping I could learn to play."

Pa Franklin snorted. "Hope in vain, girl! I heared you pound on that piano, and you ain't got a lick of talent. Even if you did, a piano is a frill your mama can't afford."

Halley turned to Kate. "Mama, don't let him do this."

"You don't get no say," Pa Franklin said. "Have respect for your elders. Children are to be seen and not heard."

Desperate, Halley took her mother's hands. "Mama, we just lost Daddy. We can't give up everything else too."

Kate pulled her hands away and took a long shuddering breath. "Halley, we can't count on help from nobody but Ma and Pa. Counting on what people *might* do is foolish. You can't even count on what they *say* they'll do. Everybody has to look after their own folks. We have to take what's sure."

Kate turned to her father. "Well, you win. We'll sell the place and go live with you. But I'm keeping my sewing machine."

"And the piano," Halley said.

For a moment Kate hesitated, but then she said, "I'm sorry, Halley. A piano can't make our clothes or feed us."

"But Mama, Daddy always said music feeds the soul!"

Pa Franklin grunted. "Any God-fearing Christian knows scripture is what feeds the soul. Doing the will of God feeds the soul!"

Kate put an arm around Halley's waist. "The piano goes. Beggars can't be choosers."

Pa Franklin nodded. "Now you're seeing reason." He glanced toward the road where a car had just pulled into sight. "Here come some folks now."

"It's Garnetta Miller!" yelled Robbie from the porch.

Halley let out her breath in disappointment. She'd been hoping for Claude or Clyde.

Pa Franklin was disappointed too, but his wife was downright riled. She had a hard time forgiving the woman who had been Pa Franklin's first sweetheart many years before. Despite four marriages and three divorces over the years, Garnetta dressed, looked, and acted years younger than Ma Franklin.

"What's that woman doing here?" Ma Franklin demanded. "It was bad enough, her coming to the funeral, and her a

Catholic. And I see she's got on one of her flashy dresses. She goes rollicking all over the country in that car, like a man. And there she goes, hugging up the boy like he's *hers*."

Sure enough, Garnetta and Robbie were embracing as if they were mother and son. The Franklins still had sour faces when Garnetta entered the kitchen. As soon as greetings were exchanged, Garnetta turned to Kate. "Have you thought about my invitation, to move in with me?"

A look of surprise crossed Pa Franklin's face. He recovered fast. "Thought about it and turning it down," he said. "My daughter's got kin."

"*Blood* kin," Ma Franklin added.

Kate said nothing, and after a moment, Garnetta said, "Well, at least let Robbie stay with me a month or two. I have a piano, and I can get him lessons. I'd bring him to see you once a week."

"No," said Pa Franklin. "The boy's place is with family."

Garnetta kept her eyes on Kate. "I can't let him go," Kate said at last. "But you'll be welcome to come visit, over in Belton."

Ma Franklin let out a disgusted huff of air, but before she could speak, a truck came into sight. It was Bud Gravitt and his family. Halley couldn't believe Orrie Gravitt would close up the store to come in person.

Garnetta headed for the pasture with Robbie and Buck as soon as she greeted the new arrivals.

Skinny Orrie Gravitt wore one of her church hats, which didn't look too fitting with the apron that she wore in a vain attempt to hide the baby she was expecting. She was so skinny that her pregnant stomach looked like she'd swallowed a huge watermelon. Bud wore work overalls and a straw hat. The Gravitt boys were probably at home, working, but Annabel and her older sister, Lula May, sat in back. Like their mother, they were dressed in church clothes.

"Me and Orrie thought we'd take a look at what all is up for sale," Bud Gravitt said.

Annabel Gravitt tugged at her mother's arm. "Yonder comes the Woodalls."

With mixed feelings Halley saw her best friend, Dimple Woodall, in the wagon. It might be her last chance to see Dimple before moving, but she hated for her friend to see their things being pawed over and sold.

"I'm speaking up for the piano first," Orrie Gravitt said to Kate. "And I might want them rockers on the porch, if the price is right. It ain't good for me to do all the standing I do."

Halley dropped down into the nearest rocker. "Daddy built these . . ."

"Halley!" Kate said. "Get up and let the grown folks sit." She turned back to Orrie Gravitt, who was now examining the washpot next to the porch. "We'll be keeping the rockers and the wash pot."

Halley went to the far end of the porch.

The Woodall wagon pulled to a stop and Dimple got out. She moved toward the end of the porch with an unfamiliar swinging gait. Her head was thrown back and her flat chest thrust out.

"Did I remind you of Bootsie Hawkins just then?" Dimple whispered when she sat down.

Halley shook her head. Bootsie had been the best-looking girl in Alpha Springs before she moved to Belton with her mother and sister a few months ago. "Neither of us is ever going to look like her," Halley said.

Dimple nodded cheerfully. "Either you got it or you ain't, I reckon. But guess what? I just got word that Lollie Marchman, of all people, got married to Rabbit Burnett. And she ain't even pretty. Runs too fat around the middle like her daddy, and she's got them little squinchy eyes and her flat rear end looks like somebody done beat the daylights out of it with a board. But here she is, married, and you and me still looking."

Halley shrugged. Lately all Dimple studied was boys.

Dimple glanced toward the pasture, spotted Robbie and Garnetta and changed subjects. "Garnetta told me she's planning on you and me helping her hunt ginseng again this fall like last year and year before last," she whispered into Halley's ear. The ginseng hunts and the money they earned from the sale of the roots were big secrets.

Halley shook her head sadly. "I'll be over in Belton."

"Well, at least you don't need the money like I do," said Dimple, "since you ain't never spent a penny of yours."

"It was supposed to be for school," Halley murmured. Her father had kept *talking* about high school for her, but Halley had known that if she herself could not find the way to pay for a ride to Jasper every day and books for all her classes, she probably would not get to go. So she had saved every penny of the fifty dollars and seventy-five cents she'd earned from two years of Ginseng hunts.

"*My* money went as fast as I got it," Dimple went on. "Shoes ever' fall and a new dress for Mama and me. I paid about all the rest on our bill at Gravitt's Store."

Halley felt a pang of guilt. The Owenbys owed some money at Gravitt's too, but Halley had never considered paying it off with her money. Nor had she put anything into the kitchen cash drawer.

More people arrived and swarmed through the house. Some children started banging on the piano.

"I sure am sorry you're leaving," Dimple said. "I won't have nobody to walk with on rolling store day." The road that went by the Owenby and Woodall places had become so washed out and rutted that the little store built on the back of a truck refused to go that way anymore. Halley didn't mind too much because she enjoyed the walk to the Freeman House. She and Dimple made it an outing. They usually took a chicken or two to trade for the few things they bought.

"When I met the store last Thursday I seen the picture woman," Dimple said.

"That woman that's got a house on a truck sort of like a rolling store?" asked Halley.

Dimple nodded. "Theodora Langford. She was wearing pants and taking pictures of ever'thing and ever'body. Somebody said she took a picture of Miz Wimpy punching down clothes in a wash pot, and Lord knows that sight's common as dirt."

Ma Franklin broke into their conversation. "Make yourself useful, girl. Draw some water."

The piano banging grew louder while Halley drew the water. There was a key to lock the piano lid down, but Halley wasn't about to give her grandfather any relief. As she set the water on the shelf next to the kitchen door, two boys began arguing over whose turn it was to spin on the piano stool. Halley rejoined Dimple at the end of the porch and a moment later the stool crashed to the floor. One boy let out a howl and several others hooted with laughter.

Dimple snickered. "Serves 'im right!"

Suddenly Halley saw her cousin Frank Earl coming, and she forgot the piano. Her heart lifted. Claude and Clyde had worked out a plan. That's what Frank Earl was coming to say. Surely it wasn't too late to cancel any sales Pa Franklin had made.

Hurry, Halley thought, jumping to her feet. *Hurry!* At this very moment Lum Albert was bargaining with Pa Franklin over livestock.

Frank Earl stopped in front of her and seemed to be struck dumb. "Pa couldn't come," he said at last. "But him and Clyde sent this." Fumbling in his pocket, he pulled out a wad of folded bills. "It's eighteen dollars. Give it to your ma when Old Man Franklin ain't around, on account if'n he sees it, he'll take it."

"Thank you," said Halley. She stuffed the money into her pocket and waited for him to go on. "And?" she said to encourage him.

Frank Earl cleared his throat and dropped his eyes. "Pa said it's best for you and your ma to move in with the preacher."

Halley flew mad. "Best for who? Best for your pa maybe, 'cause then he won't have to bother with us."

Frank Earl blushed. "Pa's going to be mighty busy working our land." He dropped his voice. "Especially now that him and Clyde are giving up the business. Say they ain't got the heart for it no more."

"Too bad they didn't decide that before my daddy got killed helping them," Halley said, dropping back down on the porch.

Frank Earl plowed on doggedly. "Pa says you won't be with Old Man Franklin long. He says Aunt Kate is good-looking enough to get another man."

Halley leaped to her feet again, fists clenched. Startled, Frank Earl almost fell backwards. "You can just go home if that's the kind of talk you're going to be having!"

Frank Earl shuffled about, obviously searching for something to say. Halley took no pity. "If it hadn't been for Claude and Clyde and their worthless truck, my father would still be living."

Lum Albert led the mules by the porch and they hee-hawed as though in goodbye. Halley put her head down on her knees. Her eyes burned with all the tears she'd shed in the last two days and all she was holding back. She heard the Gravitts moving the piano out of the house and onto the truck, but did not look.

Suddenly Dimple nudged her and whispered, "Ma and Pa are leaving. Here, this is for you." She slipped a paper bag into Halley's hand. "It's to remember me by. I bought it with the last of my gin . . . I mean, my money from Garnetta." Dimple gave her a quick hug and was gone.

It wasn't until the Woodall wagon was out of sight that Halley opened the bag. It was a diary with red binding and a locked clasp. A key on a ribbon dangled from the clasp. Slowly Halley unlocked it. When the book popped open and she lifted the cover, she had another surprise. It wasn't a diary at all. It was hollow. It was intended as a hiding place for valuables. As if she'd ever have valuables.

Halley locked the book and returned it to the bag. Everyone was loading up to leave now. Halley watched them mournfully until everyone was gone but Garnetta. She and Robbie were sitting in Garnetta's car, talking.

Halley drifted toward the kitchen where the adults were counting money. After enough was set aside to pay all that was owed, there remained only a small stack of bills and a little change. Kate reached for it but Pa Franklin was faster. He swept it up and pocketed it.

"Feeding young'uns is going to cost plenty," he said. "Get ever'thing packed, Kate. If'n it ain't raining, Ralph and Gid will be here day after tomorrow to load up what you got left. I have to get home. I got church matters to take care of."

2. Moving

"By and by, when the morning comes, when the saints of God are gathering home," Gid sang from the driver's seat of the wagon that was taking Halley and Robbie from Alpha Springs to Belton, Georgia. Her uncle had been singing the song over and over during the several hours they'd been riding, and Halley knew why. It was one of the songs Bootsie Hawkins sang. Like every other young man who saw her curvy figure and bouncy red curls, Gid was in love.

"Wish I had Bootsie here to pick on her guitar for me," Gid called from the front of the wagon. Though Halley could not see him for the household goods piled high between them, she could hear the smile in his voice.

"Bootsie's broke up with that good-for-nothing she's been going with," Gid added. "I got a chance now." He broke into song again.

"I guess Mama's already at Pa Franklin's house," Robbie said.

"Been there for hours!" Halley answered. Kate and her parents had ridden in the truck with Ralph. The hogs and chickens were in the back of the truck, along with some of the farm equipment Pa Franklin had decided to keep.

Halley had another pang of sadness. From the moment she got on the wagon, she had longed to tell Gid to stop, to take her back home and leave her. But it was no longer their home, she kept reminding herself. It now belonged to the Gravitts. Bud Gravitt would probably have a sharecropper moved into the place by next month. In a few weeks Halley's friends would forget her. Dimple would get a new best friend, her last year's teacher, Miss Henry, would be lending books to another promising student, and life in Alpha Springs would go on as if Halley had never lived there.

As they jolted along the curving mountain roads, Halley nursed her anger at her mother for accepting this total change in their life without a fight. All Kate did was pray. Even Robbie seemed to have given in to the move once Garnetta had assured him she would visit. This, too, seemed like a betrayal. Young though he was, Robbie should have some loyalty.

Gid pulled the wagon off the road one more time to let an oncoming car pass. The closer they came to Belton, the more traffic they met. The Franklins only lived in the next county, but it could have been another state, so different it was from Alpha Springs. The soil did not have the red color Halley was accustomed to. The land was flatter and less rocky. There were more houses, too.

She saw more and more of Pa Franklin's Jesus messages along the way. Crosses and signs marked every crossroad and many trees in between. "Where will you spend eternity?" they asked. "John 3:16," they said. His favorite seemed to be, "Are you ready for the Rapture?"

Halley and Robbie sat on the back of the wagon, leaning against the box containing the few books Halley owned. Buck lay between them, sound asleep. Sometimes he snored.

"Don't you reckon Pa Franklin will let me keep Buck?" Robbie whispered as though to keep the dog from hearing. It was at least the fifth time he'd asked, and every time he whispered.

Halley couldn't give him false hope, and, besides, she wasn't feeling very good toward him right now. "I don't know," she said. "But Pa Franklin told you to leave the dog. That's the last thing he said before he got in the truck to leave."

"I tried, but Buck wouldn't stay. He followed us. You seen 'im."

"*Saw* him," Halley corrected.

"Saw 'im. And I didn't let him get in the wagon until we turned on County Road Eight, and I seen—I mean, *saw*—he wouldn't go back. Pa Franklin wouldn't take 'im back to Alpha Springs, would he?"

Halley softened. She couldn't tell Robbie that their grandfather might do worse. Instead, she said, "Well, let's worry about that when the time comes."

The trouble was, the time had almost come. They were riding on pavement now, instead of dirt. Presently Halley smelled the oil and lint of the Belton Mills. Then came mill buildings themselves and the roar and clank of machinery. How could people bear working in such a place day after day, she wondered.

It was dangerous, too. Even in Alpha Springs, they heard about mill workers losing their hearing, women getting terrible injuries when their hair caught in the machinery, and men losing fingers or even entire hands.

They passed the mill village, where dozens of identical houses lined narrow side streets. They were far nicer than the Owenby house, but they were so crowded together. Children were played in the streets because the yards were so tiny.

"Over there to the left is the high school, Halley," called Gid from the front of the wagon. "That's where you'll be going to school in a few weeks."

Halley looked at the two story brick building and felt utter dismay. It was so big and so grand. At that moment, two town girls walked by. They were dressed in city clothes and their hair was curled. As though they felt her gaze, the two girls looked at Halley and then at the wagon. They laughed.

Robbie waved and hollered, "Hey!" The girls laughed again.

Halley felt her face burn. She would have to go to school with girls like this every day. Most of them would look down their noses at her. But if she wanted an education, she had to learn to bear it.

"Only a few miles more and we'll be home," Gid called from the front.

"*You'll* be home," Halley muttered. "*I* won't."

"I'm stopping at Shropshire's Store to get me some hair tonic. You young'uns stay with the wagon."

He didn't have to tell Halley twice. She didn't want to risk running into any more girls like those she'd just seen. She'd have to face them soon enough.

Gid pulled to a stop at a brick building with a tall front. Several young women and two young men were out next to the gas pumps.

Gid jumped down from the wagon and paused in the shade of a nearby oak. Slicking back his hair with a comb, he dusted his brogans on the back of his legs in a way that reminded Halley of Dimple primping to meet a crowd. Then he tucked his shirt down into his overalls. His thin body looked lost in the baggy clothes. He dug in his pockets and frowned at the coins he brought out. Shrugging, he returned them to his pocket, and then swaggered toward the group.

"Gid is here, girls!" he called. "Your prayers are answered."

"Don't sound like an answered prayer to me," drawled one of the young men. The girls giggled in the same way the two town girls had. Halley decided she didn't like them.

"More like punishment, I'd say," the other young man added. "You girls been bad?"

More giggles.

Gid played along with the teasing. "I see right now I'm gonna have to mark all you girls off my list for the Saturday night dance in favor of this other young lady I got in mind."

At that moment a car pulled up. "Bootsie!" one of the girls squealed.

It was Bootsie, all right, and the young man beside her had to be her boyfriend, Stan Duncan. Gid's face sagged with disappointment.

"Hey, Gid!" Bootsie called. "How you doing, you good-looking thing?"

Gid did not answer. Turning on his heel, he headed into the store.

Bootsie watched him for a moment and then she got out of the car slowly. Though she wasn't obviously made up and her dress wasn't overly tight, somehow her curves, her blazing hair, and her generous bosom defeated any attempt to tone them down. Her full lips and sparkling green eyes made face paint unnecessary. The girls at the gas pump looked at her in envy while the young men squared their shoulders and slicked their hair.

Bootsie spotted Halley and waved. "Hey!" she called, hurrying over to the wagon. She was smoking a cigarette, Halley noticed, and her nails were painted bright red. Bootsie gave Halley and Robbie each a one arm hug. Then she petted Buck. "Pretty dog."

"He's smart, too," Robbie said.

"I bet." Bootsie cast an eye at all the furniture and boxes on the wagon. "Moving?"

Halley nodded. "We've got to live with Pa Franklin. He thinks we can't live in our house without a man."

"I know how that story goes," Bootsie replied. "People

talk. That's why Mama decided to move us over here." She dropped the cigarette and ground it out with her foot. "I was real sorry about your father, Halley. He was a good man."

Halley nodded and blinked away tears.

"I wanted to go to the funeral real bad after word got out," Bootsie went on. "But Stan wouldn't take me, and it was too late to find another ride. Fact is, I had a big fight with Stan over that."

So that's what the break-up was about, Halley thought. At least Bootsie's heart was in the right place.

"Wasn't until today that I give 'im a chance to explain. Turns out, Stan was just too broke up about it. Stan's real tender-hearted, and funerals just break his heart. I felt like a worm when he explained. I never thought of that." She could not meet Halley's eyes.

Halley was embarrassed. It was an obvious lie. Stan had never laid eyes on her father. She struggled to find a response and finally said, "I understand."

"Well, anyway, I guess my wedding is on again," Bootsie said.

"You're marrying Stan?"

Bootsie nodded. "But don't tell nobody. Stan wants to keep it a big secret for right now. He goes to college and wants to wait 'til he finishes out this year. Oh, Halley, I sure am glad I'm not marrying an old man like Elsie did."

"Elsie's married?" Halley hadn't heard this.

"Uh-huh. Her husband, Tom Belcher, is older than *Mama*. He works for the railroad. I think Elsie just married him so we could have a man in the house and be respectable. Elsie and Mama both work at the mill, and I'm about to hire on myself."

"You dread it?" Halley had to ask.

Bootsie shrugged. "I druther work there than slave from

daylight to dark in the field. Course I guess I'll quit once I'm married. Stan's pa is the mill manager, and I guess Stan will work for him somehow."

"Bootsie," called Stan. "I got our cold drinks. Let's go."

"Just a minute, hon," she called. Then she said to Halley, "When I get to be a full hand at the mill, I'll speak for you a job. See you around." Moments later Bootsie was in the car with Stan, and they sped off.

"You going to work in the mill?" Robbie asked.

Halley shuddered. "I hope not," was all she could say. Her world had changed so much in only a few days that nothing seemed sure anymore.

Soon Gid returned. His face was long and gloomy. He tossed them each a peppermint stick, and then paused to look at Buck. "Surprised Pa let you bring that dog. Pa's dog, Goliath, don't take to strange dogs on the place."

Robbie flinched and grabbed Buck in a tight hold. When the wagon was moving again, he whispered, "Old Goliath better not fool with my dog."

"I told you we should give Buck to Garnetta or the Woodalls," Halley said. Why hadn't she been more firm?

"Nobody's taking my dog," Robbie said. "Nobody."

There was no point in arguing. They would just have to live with whatever happened now.

They crossed over the railroad tracks and Gid called back, "There's a hobo jungle down there to the right. They say that woman picture-taker's been down there with her camera, but y'all stay away. I think most of the tramps are just hungry, broke men looking for work, but it don't hurt to be careful."

The wagon rolled on, and they soon left the noise and smells of the mill behind. The pavement ended and the houses scattered into farmland once more. Pa Franklin's Jesus signs became more and more frequent. Robbie finished off his candy stick and then began on Halley's.

"Your school house, Robbie," Gid called from the front, and Halley and Robbie saw a one-room building off to the left.

A little later Gid called, "The colored school." This building, on the right side of the road, seemed to tilt to one side. "That road just beyond it goes to the Gowder place. They're colored folks. Make pottery—real good pottery."

Past the Gowder road and on a bit came the cut-off to Pa Franklin's house. It had two Jesus messages on either side. They turned and rolled between Pa Franklin's apple orchard and his corn field. They came to the pasture, and Halley glimpsed the pond at the lower end. A number of willow trees circled the water, along with patches of blackberry brambles. The wall of dirt which dammed it on the downhill side had grass and sumac growing on it. A worn cow path traced its center. Something else to warn Robbie about.

Turning from the pond, she looked at the house that was to be her home whether she liked it or not. A gray, unpainted house–much like the Owenby house–it had an open dogtrot hallway down the center. On either side of that hallway were two large rooms that opened into each other. The hallway ended on the front and back at large porches. The back porch had a fifth room, called the far room, on one end. This room would now belong to Halley, Robbie, and their mother.

Pa Franklin and Ralph waited on the front porch. Ralph was a younger version of his father in appearance but he had a much milder disposition. He never raised his voice. With them was the largest dog Halley had ever seen. He broke into a volley of barking that made Buck crawl between a mattress and a dresser.

Pa Franklin silenced the dog with one brisk order. "Hush!"

The dog obeyed, but remained alert, his twitching nose directed toward the wagon. Fur was raised on the back of his neck.

"You took your time," Pa Franklin said to Gid. "Ralph has been needing to get home, and he can't until he helps you unload." Quietly, Goliath eased off the porch while Pa Franklin's attention was diverted.

The old man turned to Halley. "You, girl," he began, but the order was cut short when Goliath suddenly lunged at the wagon with bared fangs and furious growls. Robbie jumped up, grabbed Buck, and backed into the tight space the dog had found.

"Here, Golly!" Pa Franklin ordered. "Here!"

Reluctantly, the dog obeyed. When he was lying on the porch, Pa Franklin turned on Halley and Robbie. "What's that mutt doing here? You disobeyed. Didn't I tell you to leave that dog at your house?"

"I did leave him," Robbie protested, "but he followed us."

"That's right," Halley hurriedly agreed. "Robbie didn't let Buck on the wagon for several miles."

Kate and Ma Franklin came out on the porch, and, though she knew it was hopeless, Halley turned to her mother. Kate looked sorrowful, but her arms were folded across her chest in a desperate hug. "You must obey," she said at last.

Pa Franklin turned on Gid. "And where was you when all this was a-happening?"

"Gid didn't know anything about it," Halley replied before Gid could defend himself. "He didn't hear you say Buck couldn't come, and he didn't know when Buck jumped on the wagon."

"Right there is the trouble," said Pa Franklin. "Gid never knows or hears anything he's *supposed* to know or hear."

"Now, Pa," Ralph began in a peacemaking tone, "no big harm done."

Pa Franklin ignored him.

Gid didn't appear to be taking his father's words too seriously. Calmly, he began to untie the ropes that held all the furniture and household goods in place on the wagon.

This seemed to fan Pa Franklin's wrath. "If Gid would get his mind on something other than loose women and running to dances," Pa Franklin continued, "he might be able to do what he's supposed to do once in a while! For one example, right now he needs to pull this wagon around to the back porch before he gets ready to untie ropes."

Gid began humming under his breath.

"Tie the dog up, Gid," Pa Franklin said, "and when the furniture is in and set up, you can take him off and get shut of him." When Gid did not instantly obey, he added, "Or I can get my shotgun and take care of it here and now."

Gid moved to take the dog from Robbie. Halley held her sobbing brother while Buck was forced from his arms.

"We don't allow no fits to be pitched around here," said Pa Franklin, striding toward Robbie, one hand fumbling with his belt.

Ralph moved faster and took Robbie from Halley. "I'll handle this, Pa," he said.

Halley ran after Gid. She caught him at the barn where he was tying Buck in an empty stall. "What are you going to do with Buck?"

"You don't want to know," he replied.

Buck gave out a mournful howl.

"Can't you find somebody who'd give him a home?"

Gid snorted. "Not lessen we can call down a miracle and change him into the best hunting dog in the country. Trouble is, people that want dogs already got dogs. And them people don't want another'n to feed. Most folks hereabout barely got food enough for their family these days."

"Maybe Ralph," Halley suggested.

"Not a chance. His wife hates dogs."

"How about Bootsie? She liked Buck when she saw him while ago."

Gid didn't answer, but she saw his eyes flash at Bootsie's name. He pushed the stall door shut and secured it with wire.

Halley persisted. "You know where Bootsie lives?"

Gid nodded.

"Gid," called Pa Franklin from the house, "quit dragging your tail and get back here. Ralph has pulled the wagon up to the far room. He can't unload by hisself."

"Coming," Gid answered. To Halley, he said, "Won't hurt to ask Bootsie. It's a good excuse to go see her."

With that Halley had to be satisfied.

<hr />

3. The Calvins

HALLEY, ROBBIE, AND KATE WERE SOON SETTLED INTO THE FAR room. The room had been empty since the older Franklin children had moved away. Robbie's small cot was in one corner, and Halley shared a full-size bed with her mother. What few of their household possessions Pa Franklin had not sold were in the room, but it seemed bare and ugly when Halley opened her eyes the morning after their first night under the Franklin roof.

At first, she did not know what had wakened her. Then she realized that a kerosene lamp was lit in one corner of the room, and Kate was kneeling nearby, praying softly. It scared Halley to see her mother so absorbed in trying to get to heaven, when Halley and Robbie needed her so much in this world.

Even as she watched, Kate stood and smoothed her dress and apron. "Halley," she called. "Gid has probably finished milking. Hurry and take the fresh milk to the spring and bring last night's for breakfast."

Kate shook Robbie. "Out of bed. Your job is to fill the wood box. Step lively, both of you. I don't want Pa saying we're not pulling our weight."

"He'll say that anyway," Halley answered.

Halley got up. Stepping out of the lamplight, into the shadows, she shucked her gown, found her clothes from yesterday and pulled them on. She was in a hurry to catch Gid while he was alone in the barn. He had left with Buck right after supper last night, and, much to Pa Franklin's chagrin, had not returned at bedtime.

Pulling her box of books from under the bed, Halley felt underneath the stacks until she found the diary from Dimple. From her bosom, she pulled the ribbon with the key on the end and unlocked the clasp. Running her hand into the partially opened box, she felt the folded bills and coins that, with Claude and Clyde's money gift, added up to seventy dollars and seventy-five cents. If Kate knew about the money from Jim's brothers, Pa Franklin would know, and if he knew, he would take it. Halley didn't intend that to happen. That money, plus her ginseng earnings, was all the Owenby family had.

Halley's fingers found three quarters among the coins.

Closing the box, she locked it and put the quarters in her pocket. The key she returned to her bosom. She made sure to put the diary underneath a stack of books before sliding the box back under the bed.

"What you doing?" asked Robbie in a sleepy voice.

"Just putting my night clothes away," she said and laid her folded nightgown on top of the books. "You better get up now."

GID WAS TOSSING HAY down to the mules when Halley entered the barn a few minutes later. It was still so dark that she could hardly see him moving about up in the loft. She could smell the musty, dusty smell of hay, though, and hear the swishy thunks it made when it landed in the feed bins. Gid was whistling—a good sign, she thought.

"Morning, Gid," Halley called. "Did you see Bootsie last night?"

"Sure did."

"What did she say?"

"Said I was the sweetest boy she knowed."

Halley grunted impatiently. "You know what I mean! What did she say about . . ." She paused to look around quickly, and saw Goliath skulking behind her with suspicious eyes. "What did she say about Buck?"

"Said no."

"I've got a little money to go toward feed if you think that'd change her mind," Halley quickly offered, fingering the quarters in her pocket.

"Let me finish," said Gid. "Bootsie's sister come out on the porch and seen Buck do his tricks. She took on about the way he could set up and beg. Then she said her husband Tom's been looking for a railroad dog ever since his old one died."

"Railroad dog?" Halley had never heard of such.

"Some of the railroad people keep a pet that makes all the runs with 'em. Mostly it's dogs but she said Tom'd heard tell of one railroad *cat*."

"And the railroad bosses allow it?"

Gid laughed. "I spect the higher ups don't even know about it. So if Tom takes a shine to 'im, old Buck would get to travel the country right there in the train cab, and he'd eat whatever the workers eat. He'd have his living *made*. Can you beat that?"

Halley let out a happy sigh. At least the family dog might get a happy ending. "Thank you, Gid," she said and ran to get the milk.

Breakfast was skimpy—biscuits, gravy, and coffee or milk for everyone. In addition to this, Gid and Pa Franklin each had an egg and two thin slices of fried salt pork.

"We're working," Pa Franklin explained when he saw Robbie's eyes on his plate. "When you're doing a man's work, you'll get fed like a man."

Robbie did not complain. His spirits were high since Halley had passed on the possible good news about Buck. Though she had warned against counting on it, Robbie had soon convinced himself that Buck was born to be a railroad dog.

As he ate, Pa Franklin laid out the day's work. "We're going to pull corn in the south field," he said to Gid, "and we've got to fix that buggy wheel too."

"Good," said Gid. "I'll need it fixed for Saturday by dinner, when I aim to quit work."

"I ain't fixing that buggy so's you can loafer all over the country while work here goes undone."

"I'm twenty, Pa. Plenty old enough to court girls."

"Run with sorry girls, you mean, like that Hawkins girl. Ain't no decent girls hanging around them dances you go to.

You going to have to build you a shed back behind the house and do your own cooking and washing if'n you fool around and catch a bad disease."

Robbie put down his fork. "What's a bad disease?"

"Eat and keep quiet," Kate said.

"We seen Luke Calvin and his family yesterday in Belton," Pa Franklin said after a while.

"Him and all them fine-looking daughters of his'n," said Ma Franklin. "That Clarice is pretty as a picture."

Gid rolled his eyes. "Do tell."

"Luke says Old Man Samson is about to have his first cotton come in," Pa Franklin continued. "Kate, I told Luke that you and the young'uns would hire on along with me."

"Very well, Pa," said Kate.

Pa Franklin turned stern eyes on Halley and Robbie. "Ever'body's got to earn their keep. These are hard times."

"Especially in this house," said Gid.

Pa Franklin looked at Kate. "Bernice Mitman can help you get on at the mill. You go see her, and she'd learn you what she knows about being a weaver."

"Yes, sir," Kate said.

Halley's heart sank. Mama working in that dangerous place!

Catching his father's eye averted, Gid sandwiched a slice of his pork into a biscuit and slipped it onto Robbie's plate. He put a finger to his lips and grinned.

Ma Franklin was watching the entire time and Halley feared she'd tell, but she remained silent.

Pa Franklin took a drink of coffee and frowned at Kate. "You must've made this coffee. It's weak as cat piss."

"Mama don't allow us to use that word," Robbie said, turning to his mother for support.

"Not a thing wrong with calling a thing what it is," Pa

Franklin said. "And quit talking with your mouth full."

"I was trying to be saving with coffee," Kate said. "It's thirty-eight cents a pound."

"Save somewhere else," he replied. "I can't abide weak coffee."

There was a silence for a few minutes, and then Ma Franklin smiled across the table at Gid. "Since you're bound and determined to loafer on Saturday, I tell you where you can go in that buggy. Miz Calvin told us yesterday that her high faluting sister in Atlanta sent a big box of hand-me-downs, and she said Kate's young'uns could help their selves. You could go over there and set a spell and then fetch the clothes."

"Forget it, Ma," said Gid. "I done told you to quit trying to match me up with one of them Calvin girls."

Ma Franklin bristled. "There's not a thing wrong with them girls!"

Gid downed the last of his coffee and pushed away from the table. "I didn't say there was, but I ain't interested. Let Halley and Robbie go. The clothes are for them."

In the silence that followed, Halley tried to recall the Calvin girls. She must have seen them when her family visited the Franklins and attended their church. Only a vague memory came to her.

Kate spoke. "Halley, reckon you and Robbie need to go see about the clothes today. But you better draw several tubs of water before you go. The wash needs to be done."

As soon as the breakfast dishes were finished and the water drawn, Halley and Robbie set out for the Calvin house. They were loaded down with gifts from Ma Franklin—two jars of blackberry preserves, two jars of honey, and the last of the fresh tomatoes.

Halley set a brisk pace past the pasture and the orchard,

but when they reached the main road and were out of sight, she slowed. The faster they walked, the sooner they would be back. They sidetracked into several of the cotton fields they came to and looked at the worms crawling on the cotton leaves. They searched for wild muscadines in the woods just long enough for Robbie to drop a jar of honey and break it. Then they had to stop at the creek so he could wash his feet and hands.

Soon after they left the creek a car came around the bend. Halley recognized it at once. It was Bootsie and Stan. Bootsie was snuggled right up by Stan's side and when they slowed for the curve she yelled, "Hey, Halley, Robbie."

Halley waved. It felt like Bootsie had moved on into a different world—a more dangerous world, where the rules were not clear. Halley wondered how Bootsie could trust Stan so much. I guess she's a better person than me, Halley thought.

They came to Hopewell Baptist Church. Halley would have known it was her grandfather's church even if she hadn't been visiting it all her life. The cutoff to the church and the cemetery was dotted with crosses and signs. Every tree had at least one Jesus message. Some had two or three. Wooden crosses marked some of the graves too—those without stone markers.

"You want to go in and play the piano?" she asked Robbie.

Robbie nodded eagerly.

They entered the silence of the church. It was even smaller than the Ebenezer Church in Alpha Springs. Halley sat on the first bench and listened to Robbie play "Amazing Grace."

"This old piano needs tuning worse than ours," he said.

Halley was mystified. It was as if he could understand a language she didn't, even though he was eight years younger. "How can you tell?" she asked.

"Can't you hear it?" He plunked several notes to show her.

Halley shook her head, remembering her grandfather's words about her lack of talent. Getting up, she went out to look at the graveyard.

Nobody she knew personally was buried there, but she found the graves of the two children Ma and Pa Franklin had lost in infancy long before Halley was born. The two small graves were outlined with rocks, and looked like the graves of the Owenby babies, except each had a small stone marker.

A new grave off to the edge reminded her of her father's grave in Alpha Springs. The mound of raw earth still had a few wilted flowers on it. Like her father's grave, it had no stone. Someday perhaps no one would know who was buried there.

Suddenly it seemed very important to mark her father's grave—to let the world know he had lived, and that living people missed him. She probably had enough to pay for a stone, but she couldn't buy it secretly, and if Pa Franklin discovered she had money, he would take it before she could ever buy a stone. She had to find another way.

Halley was still thinking about the stone when they left the churchyard. But when they reached the Calvin house a short while later, such thoughts were driven away. The house was big, with porches wrapping around three sides. It had a sparkling cheerfulness about it too. It wasn't just the paint. The yard was dotted with flower beds. Cactus plants were set up on posts, probably to keep children away from the prickly spines.

There were rope swings hanging from trees and a big swing on the front porch. There was a playhouse off to one side with its own little porch and windows. Halley couldn't imagine Pa Franklin taking the money, time, or effort to build something like this for his children or grandchildren.

Three girls, the youngest around Halley's age, met them on the porch. They were all plump and pretty blondes. Dimple would have died of envy if she could have seen their bosoms.

"I'm Clarice," the tallest one said. "And these are my sisters, Eva and Lacey." She turned to her sisters. "See, I told you Halley was pretty like her mother. I recollected that from when they come to our church."

Halley blushed. She wasn't accustomed to being called pretty, because she wasn't. Mainly people noticed how strong and healthy she was, or what a hard worker, or how smart she was in books. "I don't favor my mother," she said. "I'm more like my father."

Mrs. Calvin came out, and Robbie gave her the remaining jar of honey and then ran off to play with the Calvin boys, who had come from behind the house.

"Dooley, Steve!" Lacey called after them. "Show Robbie the new puppies."

"There were supposed to be two jars of honey," Halley said when she presented the preserves and tomatoes, "but Robbie dropped one."

"No one needs to know. Come in, come in. While I get dinner on, you girls go through the clothes. Pick out for your mother and brother, too."

The girls took Halley down a long hallway to what obviously was their room. There were two large beds. A dresser with a big mirror stood next to a large wardrobe with another mirror. Frilly curtains hung at the windows and colorful quilts covered the beds. Sunshine made the wide board floors gleam. It smelled like sunshine and starch and talcum powder.

Stacked on a table were some things that were not quilts, but from a distance almost looked like them. Close up, Halley could see they were fuzzy flower patterns on a fuzzy background.

"Chenille," explained Eva. "These are the tufted bedspreads we've done this week. You didn't see any before?"

Halley shook her head.

"We earn money doing 'em."

Eva pulled a box from under the bed. She showed Halley the sheets of unbleached muslin fabric with a blue design stamped on each. There was a smaller box of colored spools of yarn that had to be sewn into the designs with large needles.

"I hate clipping threads," said Lacey. "If you nip the cloth, even a little, Mr. Bonner won't pay you for the spreads."

"How much does he pay?" Halley asked eagerly.

"Different amounts," Eva replied. "Twenty-five cents for some. Thirty-five for others. Depends on the amount of work."

Before Halley could ask more, Clarice pulled her over to a big box in one corner. "Everything in here is going to look beautiful on you, with your good build."

Halley blushed. "Me? I don't have any shape at all."

"Yes, you do!" Eva said. "Little bitty waist, slim legs, and you're beginning to sprout a bosom."

Self-conscious, Halley folded her arms across her chest.

"Do you wear a brassiere?"

Halley nodded. "One I made."

"One of the bought ones in this box will do better," said Clarice. "Close the curtains, Lacey." She pulled a yellow print dress from the box. "Try this."

"We'll turn our backs 'til you're dressed," said Eva.

The girls turned away, but they continued going through the box, tossing boy clothing in one pile and girl clothing in another.

"I'm dressed," said Halley when she was buttoned up.

"Oh," said Clarice, "if only I could wear that dress and look that good. Then maybe I could catch Gid's eye."

Eva nudged Halley. "She's sweet on your uncle."

Halley could think of nothing to say.

"Little good it does me. Only one I can catch is Homer."

"I think Homer Russell is good-looking," said Eva. "I'd go with him in a minute."

Clarice took Halley by the shoulders and turned her toward the wardrobe mirror. "Look at yourself."

Halley could not believe her eyes. She looked older and prettier, and she had more shape. It made her feel good in one way, but it worried her too. She wasn't ready to look this grown-up.

"Wear that to church and you'll have a feller in no time," said Lacey.

"If there are any boys left that didn't already join the CCC," said Eva.

"CCC stands for Civilian something, something," Clarice explained when Halley looked puzzled. "It's government jobs for young men who can't find paying work. They plant trees, fill in washed-out land, clear out creeks, and stuff like that. Trouble is, the government takes the boys so far off that they can't court girls around here."

"Too bad they don't just take the sorry ones like Stan Duncan," said Eva. "Nobody'd miss him except his mama."

In response to Halley's questioning look, Clarice went on, "Never works. All Stan does is run that car of his daddy's into the ground and throw away money."

"And they say he's got two girls in trouble already," Lacey whispered.

"Let Halley try on clothes," said Clarice, changing the subject.

Halley ended up taking three dresses, two brassieres, and

two raincoats—one for her and one for her mother. There were three pairs of pants and two shirts that looked like they would fit Robbie. Halley tried to head home after she wrestled Robbie away from the puppies and determined that the clothing she had picked for him was a good enough fit, but the Calvin girls wouldn't allow it.

"We've got to show you how to tuft," Clarice insisted. Then Mrs. Calvin had dinner on the table and simply wouldn't accept a refusal to her invitation to eat.

Halley could hardly believe the feast on the table when they sat down. Chicken and dumplings and about six different fresh vegetables. For dessert, there was peach cobbler.

Robbie's eyes were large. "Ma and Pa Franklin don't ever have food like this!" he exclaimed after the blessing.

The Calvins looked at each other and Halley kicked her brother under the table. "We have enough to eat," she said.

The amount of food Robbie piled on his plate gave her the lie. He had seconds on everything, including the cobbler. As for Halley, it was the happy conversation during the meal as much as the food that she enjoyed. She hated for dinner to end, but she knew there would be trouble if she stayed much later.

"See you at church on Sunday," Clarice called as Halley and Robbie were leaving.

"See you then," Halley answered, but her mind wasn't on church or the dinner on the grounds after services. Her thoughts had returned to her father's marker. Now she knew how she could get the money for it. She was going to tuft spreads!

4. Dinner on the Ground

GID WAS AS GOOD AS HIS WORD. ON SATURDAY, DESPITE HIS father's continued objections, he quit work at dinnertime.

Meanwhile, Kate, Halley and Ma Franklin cooked for Sunday. "Webb allows me to cook plenty of vittles for dinner on the ground," Ma Franklin said. "We'll bake the cakes and pies today and fry chicken tomorrow morning."

When the baking was finished, Ma Franklin set Kate and Halley to making pear preserves while she spot-cleaned and ironed Pa Franklin's second-best white summer suit. Trim and muscular, Pa Franklin had a number of store-bought suits, and he knew he looked good in them.

Ma Franklin chuckled over her ironing. "Webb's as particular about his preaching clothes as when we was courting."

"Doesn't that bother you?" Halley asked. "I mean, him all dressed up in fancy clothes when you don't have anything nice to wear."

Ma Franklin waved away the very idea. "I don't need nothing fancy. I ain't up in front of the crowd like Webb, and Webb says people wouldn't think it was fitting for a preacher's wife. They wouldn't ever give him any love offerings if I was all decked out like a rich man's wife."

"Do they *pay* him anything?" Halley asked. "I mean, a salary?"

"Heavens no," Ma Franklin replied. "That's how we know our preachers really got called. They ain't preaching for money."

Halley laughed. "If our Methodist preacher in Alpha

Springs is doing it for money, I feel sorry for him, little as he gets."

Halley looked out the doorway and saw Robbie lining up bottles along one wall of the dogtrot hallway—milk of magnesia bottles, castor oil bottles, shoe polish bottles. There were a number of hair oil and hair tonic bottles, too. Robbie had discovered them all at the dump area back behind the barn. But bottle collecting seemed innocent enough, and he had apparently finished all his chores. The wood box was full and the yard fresh-swept. Halley told herself to quit worrying.

What she needed to put her thoughts on was tufted bedspreads. She had to explain the plan to Kate and get her support before letting the Franklins know anything. The trouble was, Ma Franklin was almost always within earshot, and, while she could be deaf as a post when she wished, the old lady's hearing was sharp when she wasn't supposed to hear.

After bath time that night, Halley finally had her chance. Robbie was already in bed asleep, and Kate and Halley were getting ready for bed.

Halley repeated all the Calvin girls had told her about tufting and described the spreads they'd finished. "Clarice and Eva say they'll teach me, and I aim to start tufting," she said.

Kate nodded. "Pa'll be glad to have more money coming in."

"*Mama*! I'm not giving him the money," Halley burst out. She looked toward the cot where Robbie was apparently fast asleep with a bottle clutched in one hand, and lowered her voice to a whisper. "I'm working to buy a tombstone for Daddy."

Kate shook her head. "Pa already said he would make a cross to mark the grave."

"Daddy wouldn't want one of those crosses," Halley snapped. "You know he wouldn't. Can't you stand up to them on this one thing?"

Kate bowed her head.

Halley took no mercy. "Pa Franklin kept all the money from our place and the animals he sold, and the equipment and the furnishings. We work here every day, and you know he'll take our cotton picking money and your mill pay. Can't I keep this money to buy a marker?"

"I'll ask," Kate finally said, "but don't count on anything."

Looking at her mother, with her hair let down for bed, made Halley think of happier times, only a couple of weeks ago when her father was living, and they had their own house. "I miss Daddy," she said. "Oh, how I wish . . ."

Kate stopped her. "Don't wish. All we got is now."

Halley was stunned. "I can't even remember?"

"No use. You can't go back," Kate said and got into bed.

Halley shook her head and then blew out the lamp. "I intend to remember."

Sunday morning came all too soon. Milking, feeding animals, cooking, and cleaning up after breakfast all had to be done same as any other day—only with fewer hands, for Gid was slow getting out of bed. When finally up, he was in a gloomy mood. Halley dared not ask if he'd seen Bootsie or found out what Tom decided about Buck. But that didn't stop Robbie.

"Is Buck riding in the train yet?" he asked when they were sitting down to breakfast.

"Yep," Gid replied. "Headed to Atlanta yesterday. Belcher said if you keep an eye out for the four o'clock train at Crider switch, you'll see your dog."

Pa Franklin let out a dismissive grunt.

Ma Franklin spoke up before he had a chance to say anything. "Everybody got church clothes ready?"

"I'm going to wear the yellow dress the Calvins gave me," Halley answered. "I ironed Robbie's best pants and shirt yesterday, and Mama's light blue dress."

Ma Franklin shook her head. "Light blue won't do a'tall. Kate's got to wear her black funeral dress. People would say she's looking for a man. After a few months it's all right to ease back into regular clothes, long as she don't get too fancy."

Gid pulled out of his gloom long enough to say, "Reckon you'll have to put away all your lace and satin stuff, Kate. And if I was you, I'd leave off all them pearls and rubies and diamonds."

AFTER BREAKFAST, WHEN THE women were frying the last of the chicken, Pa Franklin made his appearance in his white suit. His white hat he hung on a nail next to the door. He strutted about until Ma Franklin took the hint and bragged how fine he looked.

"Mules are hitched and I've pulled the wagon round," Gid called from the porch. "Ma, you ready for me to load food?"

"Just about," she answered, setting a bowl of green beans down in a washtub with a bowl of butter beans and a jar of peach pickles. Turning to Robbie, she said, "Stack wood in the dogtrot. My neck and back tell me we'll have rain tonight or tomorrow." She looked toward a window. "Hope it don't come early and ruin the church dinner."

"Dinner!" said Pa Franklin. "I'm more worried about cotton picking this week. If it rains much tonight, we'll not be able to pick tomorrow." Pa Franklin handed Halley an old quilt. "Cover the wagon seat. I don't want to dirty up my suit. Stay!" he ordered Goliath when Halley started out. "Don't let him touch that quilt. I'm not going to have dog hair and stink on my clothes."

Goliath sat down with a mournful expression and a low-pitched whine. He sounded like Buck.

Robbie must have thought so, too, for he ventured a quick, consoling pat on Golly's hindquarters as he headed for the woodshed. Golly stood and fell in step behind Robbie.

On the wagon, Gid rigged a second bench behind the one where the driver sat, and then he began loading washtubs of food. "Me and you'll have to keep these tubs from sliding about," he said to Halley.

"And your other job is to see that the boy behaves hisself," Pa Franklin said.

At last it was time to leave. Pa Franklin sat in the driver's seat, pulling his pants legs up by the creases and arranging the fabric for the least amount of wrinkles. Gid helped his mother and Kate onto the wagon, and then he sat next to Kate.

Halley missed Gid's jokes and singing but could think of nothing to cheer him. She took her seat on the end of the wagon bed, where she could keep an eye on the tubs and make sure the tablecloth covering remained in place. Robbie sat next to her, holding his favorite bottle, the one he had taken to bed last night. Why he liked this one so much was a mystery. It was a plain old shoe polish bottle that still had its bent and rusted lid. Robbie kept shaking it and trying to get the lid off. He even tried to get help from Gid, but Gid ignored him.

"Put it down 'til we get back," Halley whispered.

Robbie steadfastly refused, and she finally gave up. What could it hurt? After all, her grandfather wasn't complaining, not even when Robbie pounded the lid on the side of the wagon. Pa Franklin was busy examining the cotton fields they passed. He estimated how many days of picking each represented, and how many bales they might produce. Known far and wide as the best picker around, he was counting on being champion again this year.

"I pick just as hard for the other feller as I did for myself back when I had enough young'uns home to raise cotton," he bragged.

"And the fact that he gets paid by the pound don't have a thing in the world to do with it," Gid said.

Hopewell Church had just come into sight when disaster struck. Robbie pounded the lid of his bottle one more time and then shook it up and down extra hard. Suddenly the lid popped off and dark liquid spewed toward the front of the wagon.

"What in the name of God!" Pa Franklin roared. "Whoa!"

"Oh no," whispered Robbie, tossing the bottle into the bushes along the road bank.

Halley swung around to see her grandfather's beautiful white hat and suit speckled with black. The sprinkles had also landed on Kate, Ma Franklin, and Gid, but because their clothes were dark, the spots hardly showed.

Gid looked at his father and burst into laughter. "You look like a flock of crows with bowel trouble just flew over and emptied on you."

Robbie shrank against Halley.

At that moment a car came from behind and roared past. Dust rose and settled over them in a thick coating.

"Dag blast it!" Pa Franklin bellowed, standing and shaking his fist at the car. "What else is going to happen?"

Gid broke into fresh hoots of laughter. Pa Franklin got off the wagon, trying to dust himself off and wipe off spots of black. It was useless.

"What I'd like to know is, what *is* this stuff?" he demanded, rounding the wagon and looking at Robbie and Halley suspiciously, "and where did it come from?" Robbie shrank up smaller than ever, and Halley became busy adjusting the tablecloth over the tubs.

Gid wiped his eyes and straightened his face. "I think it dropped from this tree hanging over the road," he said. "Seems like I seen some birds fly off just after it happened."

"Shit!" said Pa Franklin. Then he looked at Robbie and said, "That's just calling a thing what it is." He sniffed at a big spot on one sleeve. "Don't stink."

"Bird poop generally don't," said Gid.

"You going to church with your suit in that mess?" Ma Franklin asked in a small voice.

Pa Franklin got back on the wagon. "No choice, woman. People are expecting me to preach, and I'm going to preach."

PA FRANKLIN PREACHED. SWEATING and red-faced, he preached and pounded the pulpit while sunshine was blotted out by clouds. He railed against drinking, gambling, and running with sorry women. He denounced laziness and idleness as the devil's playground. He condemned willful, ungrateful, disobedient, and ill-mannered children being allowed to pursue their headstrong ways without any responsible adult beating the fear of the Lord into them. Then he got started on the Rapture, and Halley groaned inwardly. Thankfully, some of the women shortened the misery. Obviously worried about rain, they began to head outside to put the food on the sawhorse-and-plank tables.

Finally the service ended and they were all outside. Pa Franklin blessed the food, and the people began to serve their plates. Children were supposed to wait until last, but Halley noticed that a bunch of untidy children were the first ones in line.

"The Logan young'uns," said Clarice Calvin. "Poor things

probably ain't had a full belly since the last church dinner."

"Their mama is expecting again, they say," said Eva.

"Elmer Logan is over there with the fellers who are trying to court," whispered Lacey. "Now, who does he think will walk with him?"

Halley glanced at the young man they indicated. Except for maybe being skinnier and perhaps a little more ragged than the rest, he didn't look that different. She served her plate and sat down with the Calvin girls on their blanket.

Young men began to single out young women for walks to the spring. "Here comes Homer," Eva whispered.

Homer approached with a shy grin. "Would you do me the honor of walking to the spring, Clarice?"

Clarice nodded, and they walked off together.

Just then there was a touch on Halley's shoulder, and she turned to see the thin young man Eva had pointed out a short while before. "I'm Elmer Logan, and I'm gonna walk you to the spring." He reached for her hand.

"No, thank you," Halley said, and tucked her hand under a fold of her dress. "I'm not thirsty."

The boy turned to leave, and Eva and Lacey broke into giggles. "Ain't *thirsty*," repeated Lacey, and Halley blushed. It was a stupid thing to say.

"I can't believe he thought you'd walk to the spring with *him*," said Eva. "Why would you walk with a *Logan*?"

Halley felt sorry for the boy. He probably heard what they said. "I'm not going to walk with anyone," she said loudly enough for his ears. "I'm not keeping company with anybody."

Thunder sounded in the distance, and people began to gather up leftover food. Halley saw Elmer Logan collecting his younger brothers and sisters and herding them toward a scrawny woman riding a baby on one hip. Halley felt a wave of pity. They looked as if they were starving. The thought suddenly came to her that her own family might have ended up like this if they'd stayed on their own place.

No, she thought. She refused to believe they could have ended up with no food. Relatives and neighbors would have helped. They would have worked hard. The Owenby family could not have ended up like that! Forcing her eyes away, she spotted her mother. Except for the baby, Kate might have been Mrs. Logan's younger sister. They both had the same defeated look.

The thunder moved closer. Trucks, cars, and wagons were pulling away. Many, including the Logans, left on foot.

"Want a ride home?" Mr. Calvin asked Pa Franklin as they were loading up. "Maybe Gid could drive the wagon home."

Pa Franklin took a look at the already overloaded truck. With the Calvins and their food, there was no room in the cab or on back. "Much obliged," he answered. "I believe we can make it 'fore the rain commences."

"Wanna bet?" said Gid in a low voice.

They were halfway home when the skies opened up.

5. Picking Cotton

"I SEEN BUCK ON THE TRAIN," ROBBIE ANNOUNCED AT SUPPER Monday night. "His head was hanging out the window. I could tell he knew me."

"So that's where you was after dinner, instead of being here to help me paint my Jesus signs," said Pa Franklin.

Fortunately for Robbie, painting a new batch of signs had put the old man in a good mood, so he didn't assign punishment.

"The rain last night worked out good," Pa Franklin declared. "Damp cotton will weigh heavier than dry. I'm hoping for a week of picking at Samson's before Calvin's cotton comes in and loses us our ride. If we can get a week of picking, I'm figuring I'll have half the money for my first *big* Jesus message."

Halley asked the question everyone else at the table was likely wondering. "Big Jesus message? What's that?"

Pa Franklin smiled. "On the way home yesterday in the rain, the Holy Spirit revealed something to me."

Gid laughed. "What—that you was wet?"

"Don't you crack jokes about the Holy Spirit!" warned Pa Franklin. "I seen I ain't been thinking big enough. I need to make my signs bigger. Lots bigger. Maybe paint 'em on the sides of barns and houses, roofs."

Gid shook his head. "Ain't nobody going to allow you to do that."

"Bet they would if I paid 'em a little bit."

Gid rolled his eyes heavenward. "Don't you think the Holy Spirit might druther you use that money to hire somebody to do the washing so your poor old wife don't have to kill herself bending over a scrub board?"

"Watch your tongue," said Pa Franklin.

Now that she knew what the cotton earnings would go toward, Halley was praying for more rain. Lots more. Her prayers were not answered, however, so they got up even earlier than usual on Tuesday so they could do the chores before heading to the Calvin place.

At breakfast Gid ruined his father's good spirits by announcing that he would be working for Ellis Cochran all week.

Pa Franklin was furious. "What?" he said. "Gid, I told you plain that we'd be picking for the Samsons."

"And I told *you* plain that I wasn't going to do it. I know exactly why you and Ma want me over there, and it ain't got much to do with picking cotton."

"I already give my word."

Gid pushed back his chair. "Well, I ain't give mine. I'm a grown man, and I figure I got the right to say where I'm going to work and where I ain't going to work. I put in five-and-a-half days a week here at home, and when I get an outside job, I give you and Ma near about ever' cent I earn. If that ain't good enough for you, maybe I need to move out."

Ma Franklin spoke up quickly. "Nobody said we don't appreciate what you do around here, Gid. Fact is, I don't know how we'd make it without you."

Gid wasn't going to be soothed or swayed. He grabbed his lunch pail, threw some biscuits in it, and left.

There was an awkward silence while his footsteps faded away. Even though he'd brought the whole thing on himself, Halley almost pitied her grandfather. It would be embarrassing to explain Gid's absence to the Calvins, who were giving them a ride to the Samson place.

Kate stood and began clearing the table. "Fix our lunch pails," she said to Halley.

"Don't bother with dishes," Ma Franklin said. "You need to get going. Daylight ain't far off, and the Calvins will go on without you if you're late."

Pa Franklin, Kate, Halley, and Robbie set out walking, each carrying their own lunch. Kate and Halley both wore long sleeves and had sunbonnets dangling on their backs. In addition, Kate wore a pair of Gid's pants to protect her legs. Halley refused to do this. "I'll be hot enough the way it is," she said.

"You'll be as tanned and scratched as a field hand," Kate warned.

"Why not?" asked Halley, dodging a mud puddle she was barely able to make out in the breaking daylight. "I *am* a field hand."

The Calvins were getting into the truck when Pa Franklin and the Owenbys arrived. Halley only had time to scrape the worst of the mud off her shoes before getting into the back of the truck with Robbie and the Calvin siblings. Robbie stood, leaning against the cab with Dooley and Steve. Halley sat nearby on a pile of pick sacks next to Clarice.

"I thought Gid was coming," Clarice said when the truck started moving.

Halley became very absorbed in grabbing for Robbie. "I think he promised somebody else."

There was an awkward silence, and then Clarice replied in a cool voice, "Well, I don't think nobody's begging him to come. I know *I* ain't. And you can tell 'im that."

"Homer Russell's been asking her to go to the picture show with him," Lacey confided, "but Clarice has been putting him off, hoping . . ."

Clarice gave her sister an elbow and a frown. "Leave the boy alone, Halley," she said as the truck hit a series of bumps and Halley grabbed one more time for Robbie. "You worry as much as an old maid school teacher. You couldn't throw that young'un off this truck if you tried."

They came to a paved road and soon they reached the beginning of Samson land. It was easy to recognize—it was the best and flattest land in the county. Much of it was rich bottomland next to the river. Long ago it had been a slave plantation, and many people said the Samsons still ran it like one.

In the early morning light Halley had a glimpse of the Samson mansion when they passed the gate. They took the next dirt road to the right and stopped at the edge of a huge cotton field, where other hands, both colored and white, had already begun picking. Across a ravine and up a little rise to the right stood the mansion. To the left, the field eventually ended at a large pasture. Straight ahead, the field sloped gradually downward to a distant line of trees marking the bank of the Coosa River. This was only one of many cotton fields the Samsons owned.

They got out of the truck and stood in the tall dewy grass along the edge of the field. Halley's dress was soon wet and slapping against her legs. Two empty cotton wagons were parked next to the road just waiting for the bags of picked cotton, and at the nearest one a sour faced man was setting up a scale.

"The foreman," Clarice whispered. "Mr. Huff."

"Where's that piano music coming from?" asked Robbie.

Trust Robbie to notice that. Halley had to listen hard to make it out. It *was* piano music, though no tune she'd ever heard.

"Get your mind off music, boy," Pa Franklin said. "You're here to work."

"I'm not certain I'd call that there music," said Huff. "Mr. Samson's daughter, Amelia, is home from New York, France, and all them other places she goes. She don't play ever'day stuff. She plays stuff us ordinary folks don't know a thing in the world about—and don't *want* to know. Give me the Grand Ole Opry anytime."

Suddenly he looked around and scowled. "Tarnation! There's that poodle dog of her'n again. She can't keep ahold of it for ten minutes straight, but let it get chewed up by a real dog, and who'll get blamed?"

He ran to pick up a small white dog bedecked with ribbons on ears and tail. The dog's hair was trimmed nearly bare in some places and left in big puffs in others. It was the ugliest dog Halley had ever seen.

The man turned to Robbie. "Son, take this so-called dog up to the big house and knock on the door where the woman is playing the piano." He looked at Robbie's wet and dirty feet and legs. "Don't go inside—just wait at the door for Miss Amelia to come get the dog."

"Yes sir." Robbie took the dog and headed toward the mansion.

"Boy, you hurry back!" Pa Franklin called after him before turning to help Mr. Calvin distribute pick sacks. Halley and Kate each got a seven-footer to hook over their shoulder. Halley took Robbie's sack to hold for him. It was only four feet long, but it would not be easy for him to fill. She had picked enough to know that this first cotton would be the hardest because it grew low on the plant. You had to bend and almost squat to get it. Later, the cotton would be higher and the picking easier.

Mr. Huff decided that Dooley Calvin would be the water boy for the white workers, taking buckets of water to the different pickers about every half hour. "Here's the bucket and the dipper. You know where the spring is at, don't you?"

Naturally, Pa Franklin had to give Halley instructions before heading out on his first rows. "Leave the lunch buckets in the truck," he said, as if he'd caught her trying to snatch one. "Dinner is for dinnertime. As for the cotton, pick clean.

Don't take two rows until you can do a good job on one. Don't leave tags of cotton. Get all the cotton in one grab. Do what I say, and you'll get to be a good cotton hand."

"Robbie and I have both picked before," Halley reminded him. She could have saved her breath.

"I'm expecting you to pick your weight—or more," he went on as if she had not spoken.

Clarice rescued her. "Let's get started, Halley. The day ain't getting no younger. You can share a row with me. Eva and Lacey are picking together, and when he gets back, Robbie can share a row with Steve."

As Halley followed Clarice through the wet grass, she saw her grandfather already moving between his two rows, his hands busy. There was no wasted motion, no pauses. She supposed that's why he was so fast.

Down the field a good distance off, she saw the colored pickers. Halley stared at them curiously, especially a girl about her own age wearing a pink dress. The girl was moving down the row almost as quickly and efficiently as Pa Franklin.

"That's Opal Gowder," Clarice said. "The one with a gift."

"A gift?" asked Halley.

"She's a child who never did see her father so she can heal people, they say. I don't know how the Gowders manage to get here so early. They must come the day before and camp out in the field."

"Maybe they're kin to some of the people that work on the Samson place year-round," Eva suggested. "Could be, they stay with them during cotton picking."

Halley began to pick with energy, trying not to notice her wet skirt slapping against her legs, trying to ignore the cotton boll burrs pricking her hands. She didn't want to be shamed when the bags were weighed.

The sun came out, and the grass and cotton began drying. Dooley came with the water bucket, and Halley thought of Robbie. She looked toward the big house, and, sure enough, there he was, strolling slowly back as if there was no work to be done. Halley let out an irritated puff of air.

"Leave 'im be," said Clarice. "How's the boy ever going to learn if you spend all your time saving him?"

Forcing her eyes from Robbie, Halley went back to picking. As time passed, she found she could talk and pick at the same time. She paused from her work only when Dooley showed up with water.

"Are you and your sisters going to school this year?" she asked Clarice after she drank her fill. She had been thinking on this. If one of the Calvin girls went to the high school in Belton, then Halley would have at least one friend, and she could endure the stuck-up girls like those she'd seen in Belton the day of the move.

"Just Lacey. She says she's going to go ahead and finish eighth grade at the Springplace school before she quits. Me and Eva already quit. Mama said she couldn't see no sense in walking to school at Belton."

"I'm sorry," Halley said.

Clarice shrugged. "I'm not. Country girls don't fit in there at the town school, from what I hear. And what would I do with more schooling? Lord knows, I don't want to be a schoolteacher, which is the only thing I could do with all that learning. I sure wouldn't want to get me a camera and travel the country taking pictures like that woman people keep seeing in Belton and round about. No, thanks! I want to get married and have me a baby."

"I want to do something else before I get married," Halley said. "I want to finish high school, maybe go to college.

Maybe be a teacher or a nurse or a doctor."

Clarice was astounded. "People *talk* about nurses. I guess they'd talk about a woman doctor, too."

"Do you ever wish you lived in a place where people didn't talk so blamed much?"

Clarice laughed. "There ain't no such place, Halley, unless it's heaven, and I ain't ready to go there yet."

Finally it was dinnertime. When they weighed up and emptied their their sacks, Halley found she had sixty pounds. It was almost as much as Kate had picked, so Halley was pleased until her grandfather spoke.

"You can do better," he said, and then, with the help of Mr. Huff, he lifted his bag and caught it on the hook of the scale. Mr. Huff actually smiled. "Two hundred and two pounds," he announced. "How do you do it, Preacher Franklin?"

Pa Franklin was happy to explain. As Halley grabbed her lunch pail and headed off to a shady place near the ravine, she heard him telling how to pick with two hands.

The Calvin girls had ham in their biscuits and fried apple pies to finish off with. They insisted that they had brought extra, so Halley finally took one biscuit and a pie. Her mother, who was sitting quietly nearby, refused.

All too soon Mr. Huff bellowed, "Time to go back to work," and all the pickers trudged back into the field. The rows of cotton were shimmering in the heat. The humidity in the air grew heavier as they neared the river, but Halley's throat soon felt parched. At last she saw Dooley coming with the water bucket, and she took off her pick sack to stretch.

"Time to get back to work, girl," yelled her grandfather.

THE SUN WAS GOING down when they weighed up for the last time. Halley's legs felt too heavy to move, and her shoulder ached from the burden of the cotton sack.

"I'll be collecting the pay for my daughter and my grand-children along with mine," Pa Franklin told Mr. Huff.

They couldn't even be trusted to have the money in their pockets until they got home, Halley thought.

On the way back to the Calvin place Robbie again stood, leaning over the cab. His fingers were dancing over the metal, playing imaginary music.

Mr. Calvin took pity on them and drove on to the Franklin house.

"Git the mail, girl!" Pa Franklin called out the window when Mr. Calvin slowed to take the turn-off to the Franklin house.

Halley slid off the truck in back and Mr. Calvin went on. In the mailbox she found the very first letter from Dimple. She tore it open and read it eagerly.

Dear Halley,

I miss you. I couldn't rite til now. We didn't have no riting tablit or envelops. I boried these from Garnetta.

Molly set with a boy at church Sunday. It was Cletus Hill, but the airs she put on youd think it was the guvner.

Miz Gravitt is havin more trouble with her secret con-dition. You know what Im talking about. Turns out Lollie Marchman has the same secret condition. Rekon now we know why Rabbit Burnette married her.

Next week Garnetta wants me to help her like last yr. You know what I'm talking about. Wish you could be here,
   Love
   Dimple

Halley wished she could be there, too.

6. Tufting Spreads

They were only able to pick cotton a few days. When Luke Calvin's crop came in, his family stayed home to pick their own cotton. Pa Franklin could find no other ride to the Samson place, and no one within walking distance was hiring pickers.

"Now you've got a chance to go talk to Bernice Mitman about a weaving job at the mill," Pa Franklin said to Kate at supper after the last day of picking.

"Yes, sir," said Kate.

"Bernice worked at the mill for twenty years or more, 'til her health went bad," Pa Franklin continued.

"Probably went bad from working at the mill," Halley said.

"Had nothing to do with it," Pa Franklin said to Halley before turning back to Kate. "The more you know going in, the more apt you are to get a regular job."

"I'll go tomorrow," said Kate.

Halley had her own plans. Tuesday was Mr. Bonner's regular day to drop off stamped spreads at the Calvins. Because of cotton picking, probably only Mrs. Calvin would be at home, but that did not matter to Halley. She was eager to meet Mr. Bonner and get her first spreads.

During the night the rain started, and it was still falling the next morning. "It's messy out there," said Ma Franklin at breakfast.

"Ah, a little rain never hurt nobody," said Pa Franklin.

"Except maybe for a little pneumoney fever now and then," said Gid.

After breakfast Halley and Kate put on the raincoats from

Mrs. Calvin's sister's hand-me-down box and waited on the front porch for a break in the rain. It didn't look promising. Water poured off the roof in sheets, and the rain barrel overflowed into a yard that was like a lake.

Golly must have smelled them from the barn. He came running from that direction, jumped up on the porch, and shook himself. Kate and Halley ducked away from the water and the doggy smell. Not Robbie. He came from the kitchen and slipped Golly a biscuit—the one with Gid's meat in it.

"Can I go with you to the Calvins'?" he begged.

Before Halley could answer, Gid came down the dogtrot. He winked at Halley and said, "Robbie, I'm gonna need your help reweaving the rockers. I don't think I can spare you."

Finally, the rain let up a bit, and Kate and Halley headed out, Kate to the Mitmans' and Halley to the Calvins'. Both wore their worst shoes and carried better ones wrapped in oilcloth. They wore rain bonnets made out of oilcloth to keep their hair dry.

As they walked, Halley tried to talk her mother out of mill work.

"We have to pay our way," Kate said.

"We already *do*," answered Halley, "with all the money Pa Franklin took from us.

"Pa says different."

Halley grunted with impatience. "We'll never pay enough to satisfy him. Clarice says mill work made her mother's cousin sick—coughing up blood and such as that. And no matter what Pa Franklin says, I'll bet Bernice Mitman's ailments were caused by working at the mill."

"It's a chance I have to take."

Halley tried again. "What about that long walk to work and back every day? At least three miles each way. You'll have to walk in weather like this and on days when the ground is iced over."

"I'll manage," Kate said. "I have to."

Jut short of the Mitman cutoff, the steady drizzle became a downpour once more. "The church!" said Kate, breaking into a run. "We'll stop here and wait for the rain to slack."

Then they were inside the dimness of Hopewell Church, dripping puddles of water onto the rough floors. The building was damp and musty. The songbooks were stacked on a table near the door, and the smell of them was heavy in the air.

Halley drew her mother to a window. "See that grave right over there? The one next to the cedar tree? A marker like that is what I mean to get for Daddy."

Kate shook her head. "Don't count on it. I mentioned to Pa that you want to get up money to put a marker on Jim's grave. He thinks it's foolish."

"He put markers on his babies' graves."

"Before the Depression. Times are harder now."

"You wanted to get a marker right after Daddy died. And even a few days ago, you didn't act like it would be a bad thing to do."

Kate shrugged. "'Honor thy father and Mother.' That's what the Bible says. I have to mind Pa."

"Well, he's not my father, and I think I need to honor *my* father with a marker on his grave."

Kate frowned. "You're going to have to come down a few notches, young lady." She spoke in her father's tone of voice. "These are hard times, and they're likely to get harder. Even in good times a woman can't have everything she wants. She's lucky if she gets *anything* she wants. Getting big ideas just makes things worse."

"But Daddy always said . . ."

"Oh, Jim said plenty." Kate's voice was mocking. "'Take care of your neighbors, and they'll take care of you, get learning, and the world can be yours.' Well, he had twice as much education as me, and little good it did him. As for neighbors, I didn't see none coming to our rescue when he died."

"Don't run Daddy down," Halley cried. "Daddy was good. He was good to us."

"But like Pa says, if he'd made people pay in cash for work, if he hadn't always been handing money out to people . . ."

"That's not fair," said Halley. "*You* handed out as much as Daddy, only you gave it to preachers. And you're not fair to me and Robbie either. You don't give any notice to us. All you study is obeying Pa Franklin. If there is a God, he would want you to take care of your young'uns."

Kate drew back her hand and struck Halley's face with a resounding slap.

Halley staggered back, gasping. Her mother had never hit her before. Dodging around Kate, Halley ran to the door and out into the rain. She heard her mother call after her, but she did not reply, nor did she stop. She had left her rain bonnet, but she wasn't about to go back after it. Soon, Kate's voice faded into nothing.

A CAR WAS PARKED in front of the Calvin house. It was so loaded with sheets of unbleached muslin, yarn and other goods that there was no doubt whose it was. The Calvin dogs came around the house, and the puppies soon had Halley surrounded. Halley grabbed up a stick to use as a mud scraper, and she tried to clean her shoes, but it was hopeless. Finally, she pulled them off and was looking for a place high enough to safeguard them from the dogs when Mrs. Calvin appeared at the door.

"Scrape them on the edge of the porch and hang them on the nails next to the porch swing." she said, "Your raincoat, too."

Halley slicked the water out of her hair as best she could, and then took out her dry shoes and pulled them on before going into the house.

All the Calvin girls called greetings as she passed the door into the parlor, but Mrs. Calvin kept Halley moving.

"Halley'll be back when she gets into dry clothes," she said to her daughters. She led Halley to the girls' bedroom and found some clothes. "These will do until yours dry," she said, handing her a petticoat and dress. "My goodness whatever happened to your face?"

Halley covered her cheek with her hand. "Uh, I ran into a tree limb."

Mrs. Calvin kept looking at her for a moment and then handed her a towel and a comb. "For your hair. Come to the parlor when you get dressed."

Halley scrubbed the worst of the wetness out of her hair and then combed it. She looked like a drowned rat. A drowned rat with a red hand print on one cheek.

When Halley went into the parlor, a dark-haired man was checking the spreads the Calvin girls had tufted. A much younger man stood beside him. Both looked up as Halley entered.

"Mr. Bonner and his son, Richard," said Mrs. Calvin. "And this is Halley Owenby, the new neighbor we told you about. She moved here a few weeks ago from Alpha Springs in Bartow County."

"Oh yes," the older man said and bent over the spread again. "I know the Alpha Springs area. I've just started putting out work over there. You know the Nixons? Their oldest girl got married a few days ago."

"Mr. Bonner brings us news from all over," said Clarice.

The man handed Halley the spread he'd just been checking. "This is how your work should look."

"Father says Clarice Calvin is one of his best tufters," Richard said.

Clarice beamed.

Mr. Bonner picked up a new spread and shook out its folds. "Let's see, Alpha Springs. One of the Woodall mules died."

"Oh no," said Halley. Mules were expensive. How could the Woodalls afford a replacement?

"And Mrs. Gravitt died."

"No!" Halley was stunned. Of course Dimple had said the woman was ailing, and Halley knew women sometimes died during childbirth. But Mrs. Gravitt?

"There was a new baby born in the family before she died," Richard Bonner said.

Mr. Bonner frowned at his son for mentioning a delicate subject like childbirth in front of the young women. Then he added, "A healthy boy, they say."

Halley had never liked Mrs. Gravitt much, but the sorrow of losing her own father came back fresh when she thought of Annabel and the rest of the Gravitt children.

Mr. Bonner counted out the money due the Calvin girls and gave them all new muslin sheets with designs stamped in blue. "So you will learn to tuft with these pretty girls?" he said to Halley.

Halley nodded. "They're going to help me start today."

"You couldn't find better teachers," said Richard Bonner.

"I will give you only two spreads," said Mr. Bonner. "While you are learning. Later, maybe three or four."

Richard winked at her, and Halley blushed and dropped her eyes.

Mr. Bonner left with his son and the girls went to work. There wasn't much that they had not already shown her, and by dinnertime Halley was moving along almost as fast as Clarice. Her thoughts were moving, too. While the Calvin girls chattered and laughed, Halley was thinking about how like Pa Franklin her mother was becoming. She thought of escape, too, but the only place she could think of going was to Garnetta. Garnetta, she knew would not keep her without Kate's consent. But, even if Garnetta would take her, how could she go off and leave Robbie?

"You're awful quiet today, Halley," said Clarice at last.

"Bet she's studying on that flirty Richard Bonner," said Eva. "He's the kind to try and charm every girl he meets."

Halley's face went hot. "I was thinking about Mrs. Gravitt," she said, "and Robbie. I mean, him going to school by himself because I'll be going to school in Belton."

Eva dismissed that worry with a wave of the hand. "Steve and Dooley will take care of him. Nobody's going to pick on him long as they're around."

Halley was suddenly aware of the smell of food coming from the kitchen. She stood. "While the rain is stopped, I better change into my own clothes and head home," she said.

"Stay and eat," Clarice urged, and the other girls joined in. Mrs. Calvin heard the discussion and came to add her invitation.

But Halley insisted, so Mrs. Calvin brought her clothes, which she had dried next to the kitchen stove. When Halley had changed, Clarice handed her a bundle wrapped in oilcloth. "I wrapped your spreads and yarn, in case it commences raining again. You can return the oilcloth next week."

Mrs. Calvin handed her a paper bag, too. "A little food in case you get hungry on the way home," she said.

Their kindness almost brought Halley to tears. "Thank you," she managed to say before hurrying to the porch to change shoes. "I'll see you next week," she called as she left.

Though the rain had stopped, at least temporarily, the road was far worse than in the morning. The mud had been churned to a quagmire by the traffic of the day, and the ditches on either side were filled to overflowing. In some places, she could not go around the puddles or cross the flooded ditches to get up on the bank. In those places she had to pull off her shoes and wade. The bridge over Sipsy Creek was barely above the rushing water. The cotton fields on the downhill side of the road were partially flooded. Halley plodded on.

She came to Hopewell Church and remembered her rain bonnet. She was tempted to leave it, but then she might need it again before Sunday. Besides, now that she looked, the door of the church was ajar. There was no wagon or car in the yard—no tire or wagon tracks. Maybe Kate had left it open. Or perhaps the latch did not fully catch, and it blew open on its own.

She reached the edge of the yard and heard something from inside. Crying? She paused for a moment and then moved forward on tiptoe. Going up the steps, she peeked inside. In the dimness she saw a young woman kneeling at the altar.

"Oh Lord," she was crying, "help me! I know I ain't deserving, but please help me."

Something about the figure looked familiar. Then the girl shifted and the light from the window fell on her hair.

"Bootsie?" Halley said, stepping inside and dropping her burdens on a pew.

Bootsie turned, scrambled to her feet, and met Halley with outstretched arms. "Oh, Halley, I don't know what I'm going to do," she cried. Her eyes were puffy and her face red.

"Stan broke up with me. He said he don't want to ever see me no more."

Halley didn't know what to say. She could not be truly sorry that Bootsie was not going to marry such a lazy, selfish mama's boy. "You'll find someone else," she finally said.

Bootsie shook her head. "Nobody else will want me."

"Every young man in two counties wants you already."

"Not now." Bootsie looked back to the altar. "God don't even want me. I talked to the preacher at Mitt's Tabernacle last night. He said he didn't think I was ready to join the church."

"How would he know?" Halley burst out. "That's between you and the Lord."

Bootsie shook her head again. "The preacher said come back in six months to a year, and they'd see what kind of life I was living then."

"That's terrible!" Halley said.

"Do you think your grandfather would let me join this church?" Bootsie asked.

Reluctantly, Halley shook her head. He'd used Bootsie too many times as an example of the kind of sorry girl Gid ran after. And he'd even criticized one Belton church for allowing her to sing at the opening of revival.

Bootsie dropped down on a bench. "I don't know what I'm going to do. When not even the Lord wants me, I know for sure nobody here on earth is going to have a thing to do with me."

"I'm your friend," Halley said, "and it sure won't make me think less of you because Stan Duncan broke up with you. He's not good enough for you."

"You won't say that when you know." Bootsie looked up with despairing eyes. "Halley, I'm going to have a baby."

"Oh Bootsie!" Halley sank down on the bench beside her.

This was worse than she had imagined. "Are you sure?"

Bootsie nodded. "I didn't come around this month, and I never miss. I'm never even late. And when I told him, Stan said . . ." She broke into sobs. "He said the baby wasn't his. Said he used protection. Said his mama told him if I let him, I let other men, too. Stan knows that ain't so. He knows he was the first one—the only one. And he knows it was only after he was talking getting married that I give in."

"When I went to see old Miz Duncan this morning, I told her I'd go to court. I reckon she'll see to it I lose my job now. But I'm glad I told her. At least I got her worried. Kept saying going to court would ruin their good name and mine, too. I looked her right in the eye and I said, 'My name is already going to be mud. I ain't got a thing to lose, but you have.'"

"What are you going to do?" Halley asked.

"Keep on working, long as I have a job. Save all I can, I guess. Just wait as long as I can to tell anybody. You're the only one I've told besides Stan and his mama."

"I won't say anything," Halley promised.

"I never thought you would."

Halley reached for the paper bag Mrs. Calvin had given her. She pulled out a biscuit with a thick piece of ham in it and gave it to Bootsie and then took the second one for herself. "I never thought Stan was good enough for you. Now he's proved it."

Bootsie looked at her mournfully. "How come you could see him for what he was, and I couldn't?"

Halley shrugged. "I guess you just trust people more than I do." Two fried apple pies remained in the bag. "Here," Halley said, "you eat these. Pa Franklin will be out looking for me if I don't get home." Halley picked up her tufting bundle and retrieved her rain bonnet from the corner of the pew.

Bootsie pulled herself to her feet and together they walked outside and headed for the road. "Well, I've got to get home myself, so I can begin acting like nothing in the world is wrong."

They walked in silence for a while. When the Franklin mailbox came into sight, Bootsie asked, "Reckon you could come to see me sometime?"

"I don't think so," Halley said. "You know how my grandfather is. Well, my mother is getting more and more like him. And they have so much work loaded on me that I wouldn't have time to walk to Belton."

"Can't you go *anywhere?*"

"I guess they'll let me go to the Calvins' to get my tufting stuff once a week. Far as I know they're going to let me go to the high school in Belton. And, oh yes, Pa Franklin told me yesterday I had to clean his church on Saturdays."

"I'll come sometimes and help you," Bootsie waved goodbye and headed on toward Belton. Halley watched her and thought of the day Dimple tried to walk like Bootsie. Downcast as she was, not even Bootsie could walk like that today.

7. Gid Makes a Decision

KATE GOT THE JOB AT THE MILL THAT VERY DAY. SHE WAS TELL-ing Ma Franklin about it when Halley arrived home. Halley stood near the open kitchen window and scraped mud from her shoes.

"Bernice knew of an opening," Kate was saying, "and Bernice's boy was taking her to the doctor today, so she went by the mill and spoke for me to the foreman. When I'm a full hand, I can draw nine dollars a week."

"And be lucky if Pa Franklin lets her keep a dollar of it," Halley muttered and then went through the dogtrot to the far room. At the back porch she paused to watch Robbie and Gid in the barn shed. Robbie pulled a long oak weaving-strip from a tub of water, shook it off, and handed it to Gid while Golly watched.

"Put a few more strips in to soak, Robbie," Gid said. "Believe you and me gonna finish up before supper."

Halley went into the dimness of the far room. Only one small window and the open door to the porch provided light. Carefully, she unwrapped her stamped bedspreads and yarn. Her book box would be the best place to keep the tufting stuff, she decided. She hung Mrs. Calvin's oilcloth across the foot of the bed she shared with her mother. Ma Franklin's oilcloth, she had better return to her grandparents' bedroom. Ma Franklin didn't have much, but she was big on keeping it all in place.

Stepping out on the porch, Halley walked down the dog-trot hallway. As always, a stiff breeze stirred the air. It was nice in warm weather but would be miserable in winter. The movement of air made the hall an excellent place for drying clothes during rainy weather. For this reason lines were strung from wall to wall just above head level. Right now several dish towels and an apron hung near the kitchen door.

She came to the door to Ma and Pa Franklin's room, which was always kept closed. Halley tapped, though she could hear her grandmother talking in the kitchen. Her grandfather, she knew was gone, since his second best hat was missing from its nail just outside the kitchen door. Getting no answer, she opened the door. The storage shelves were in a corner. In front of them was strung a wire for hanging Ma Franklin's three dresses and all Pa Franklin's clothing. His suits were draped in sheets, except for the white suit with the shoe polish stains. Ma Franklin had not completely given up on it yet.

Turning to go, Halley's eyes were caught by the hearth. Around it the late afternoon sunlight showed a dusting of sand. Each room in the house except the far room had a fire-place, though none were actually used except the one in the kitchen. All the hearths were made of bricks set in sand. The sand was held by a box under the house. Halley felt a flicker of irritation. How did her grandparents manage to mess up this hearth when they never used the fireplace? Probably Pa Framlin did it on purpose to make work. When Halley was the one to sweep and mop in there, he always made sure to stand and watch until she finished.

At that very moment she heard her grandmother say, "Didn't I see that girl go by while ago? I need water."

Heaving a sigh, Halley stepped back into the dogtrot and pulled the door quietly shut. In the far room she changed into her everyday dress. Then she pulled her book box from beneath the bed. Removing the spreads and yarn, she reached underneath the books. Her diary was right where she had left it, and the clasp was still locked.

Halley hugged her knees and dropped her head. She thought of her mother working in that dangerous mill. Despite their angry words and the slap at the church, she loved her mother and didn't want her injured. Halley thought of Bootsie and the baby and wondered what on earth the girl was going to do. She thought of Mrs. Gravitt's death. Bootsie could die having her baby, she suddenly realized. The whole world seemed full of death and trouble.

Hearing footsteps, Halley shoved the book box back under the bed so hastily that she knocked against her mother's sewing basket.

Robbie entered. "I helped Gid today," he said.

"That's good," said Halley, picking up a spool of yarn with a big needle stuck in it.

"We fixed a chair, and then when it quit raining, we went to the corn mill, and then we come home and done another chair."

"Good," said Halley, spreading out the stamped muslin she'd started tufting at the Calvins.

"At the mill Gid talked to some men about a camp."

"Uh-huh." Halley examined the stitches she had already put in the spread. They seemed pretty even.

"Pa Franklin is gone to Belton."

"Good."

Robbie looked at her, a puzzled look on his face. "All you're saying is good, good. What's wrong?"

"Nothing," said Halley, reaching for her mother's sewing basket. She pulled out the scissors. "Everything's fine."

"Good," said Robbie, and he grinned.

Halley didn't feel like grinning back, and Ma Franklin

saved her the effort. "You, girl," she called. "I need water."

"Yes, ma'am!" Halley headed for the porch with the spread and yarn. Maybe she could get some work done before supper. She left her work on a rocker and then headed to the well with the water bucket.

Robbie followed, still talking. "School starts in two weeks."

School! Halley had forgotten to include homework among all the chores she must do every day before she could tuft. She might not even be able to do *two* spreads each week. Halley took the bucket to the water shelf.

"Fresh water!" she called into the kitchen and then hurried to the rocker before her mother could speak. Stabbing the needle in and out, in and out, she tried to see how much she could get done before the next interruption.

HALLEY MANAGED TO AVOID her mother until suppertime. Pa Franklin got home just as Ma Franklin and Kate were putting food on the table. The old man said his usual long grace and then, just as Halley was figuring how to tell the news about Orrie Gravitt without getting into forbidden areas, Pa Franklin saved her the trouble.

"Orrie Gravitt died," he said.

"No!" said Kate.

"Tate Shropshire says Bud Gravitt put her away first class."

Gid grunted. "That's a comfort to her, I know!"

Kate cleared her throat. "Was . . . was there a new baby?"

"A fine boy, they say."

"Lord be thanked," said Kate. "Who's taking care of it?"

"Mr. Gravitt's youngest sister. She's got a baby of her own, and milk enough to feed two."

Ma Franklin was thoughtful. "It's a blessing Gravitt's got girls big enough to take over the work of the house."

"At least Mr. Gravitt and his children won't have to leave home," Halley said.

Pa Franklin looked at her sharply. "Better count yourself lucky you got folks willing to take you in."

Gid laughed. "Not only take you in, but let you lay around in the lap of luxury."

"Kate got a job at the mill today," said Ma Franklin. "Starts Monday."

Pa Franklin's eyes lit up. "How much you making?"

"Nothing until I'm trained."

"Makes sense," said Pa Franklin, helping himself to more turnip greens and cornbread. "A feller can't pay you till you're worth something."

"The foreman asked where I live and when I told him, he said that was a long way to walk every day."

Pa Franklin snorted. "Two, three miles? That ain't nothing. A little walking never hurt nobody."

"The foreman says they've got a mill house right next to the mill, and the rent would be nearly nothing if three in the same family work for Belton."

Halley figured out where her mother was heading and added, "They have inside toilets."

"Yeah, they draw in some folks with such as that," said Pa Franklin. "*I* say, who wants to live under the same roof with a *toilet*?"

Gid spoke up. "They don't stink. Water takes the mess way off from the house."

"Might be nice in cold weather," said Ma Franklin. Then she looked at her husband's scowl and smiled apologetically. "But I reckon a chamber pot works fine."

Kate spoke hurriedly. "Pa, the mill foreman said you and Gid could hire on and we could have that house. I said I'd ask."

For once Gid and his father were in total agreement. "And give up farming?" Pa Franklin demanded. "You're a dreaming."

"Forget it, Kate," Gid said. "I ain't going to be no slave to a mill whistle, and I ain't going to suck in lint with ever breath I take."

"The foreman said we could have a garden plot behind the house," Kate continued. "Halley and Robbie could keep it going."

"Ha!" said Pa Franklin. "I hope I live to see the day when them two do enough work to earn the grub they eat! Besides ever' thing else, I can't move off and leave my church. No sir! And what about my Jesus messages? When would I have time for them? Me and Gid are staying right here, thank you just the same!"

"Speak for yourself, Pa," Gid said. "I talked to Buford Cobb again today about that CCC the government has started, and I decided to sign up. It'll be a way of earning some money, and I'm figuring to learn something else besides farming."

Ma Franklin clutched at her chest.

"Something 'sides farming?" Pa Franklin said. "What else is there that's worth doing?"

"All kinds of things," Gid answered. "CCC boys put up buildings and bridges, they learn electric wiring and fixing motors, they learn plumbing and . . ."

Ma Franklin began to cry. "You mean to tell me you'd go off and leave us with this farm to run by ourselves?"

"Try to understand, Ma," Gid pleaded. "It's time I made a life of my own. And I can still help you. The CCC will send you and Pa $25 a month. A dollar a week of that is to hire somebody to do the wash for you. Pa, you knowed I wasn't staying here forever. I already stayed longer than any of the other young'uns. *You* married by the time you was my age."

There was no reply, and after a silence Gid continued. "You be thinking of what jobs you need me to catch up before I leave. I figure it'll be a week or two 'fore I go. I'll try to get all the heavy stuff done ahead, and I aim to leave you with a shed full of split wood."

Disturbed by the loud voices, Goliath leaned in through the doorway as far as he dared.

"Out!" Pa Franklin yelled, and the dog drew back. "Reckon even my dog's trying to take it on hisself to do as he pleases."

Gid stood and headed for the porch. Soon one of the rockers began to squeak.

Pa Franklin turned on Kate. "See what you started? I take you and these young'uns in out of the goodness of my heart, and how do you repay me? You try to be the big boss. Trying to make me and Gid go to work in the mill. Then that gives Gid the big idea of joining the CCC."

Halley had to speak up. "Gid already had his mind made up about CCC before the mill jobs got mentioned."

Pa Franklin ignored Halley and kept talking to Kate. "You're so hot to get somebody else in the family on at the mill—well, you got a daughter." He jerked his head at Halley. "She's plenty big enough to start earning her keep."

"I'm going to school," Halley said.

"School?" exclaimed Pa Franklin, looking from Halley to Kate. "Surely to goodness you're not aiming to send her to school this year! She's finished with eighth grade. What does she need more book learning for?"

"I don't see much good in it myself," Kate said, "but Jim believed in it and Halley wants to go."

Pa Franklin said no more, but he set his mouth in a firm line that left no doubt as to how he felt. He got up from the table and moved out to the porch. While Halley helped clean the kitchen, she listened to the squeaking rockers. Pa Franklin and Gid were mostly silent. Only when Ma Franklin joined the men did the conversation pick up a little.

Halley and Kate did not go to the porch. They sat at the kitchen table and worked by lamplight. Halley did her tufting while Kate caught up on mending. Several times Kate looked at Halley as though to speak, but then she would only heave a sigh and go back to work.

THE MILL JOB BEGAN. Kate left home before full daylight every morning and got home when twilight was moving in. Every night her hair and clothing were frosted with lint, and she had the oily, cottony smell of the mill about her. At supper she did not talk much and when she did, it was only about the weaving job she was learning. How she had to learn to catch broken threads and tie them back in right away. How fast the cloth moved through the loom and how one thread gone wrong could ruin an entire run. How closely the boss man watched, and how easily a person could be dismissed if the supervisor was displeased. Kate's night time praying continued, to Halley's dismay. She wondered how her mother could go in to work after missing sleep for those long prayers every night.

Little more was said about the CCC in the days after Gid's announcement. It was as if Pa and Ma Franklin hoped that if they ignored it, Gid would forget all about it. Halley dreaded Gid's departure almost as much as the old folks did. Now that he was leaving, she realized all the little things Gid did and said that made the Franklin house more pleasant. She almost wished along with her grandparents that he would fail the physical examinations all CCC boys had to pass. He didn't.

All too soon came the day for Gid to leave. Kate told him good-bye before leaving for work, and the rest of them were there to see him off when his friend Buford came by. They were walking to town to catch the bus together with several other recruits.

Halley thought Gid looked a little scared, maybe a little reluctant to leave, now that the time had come. He hung back behind Buford. Pulling Halley to one side, he pressed a bill and a little change into her hand.

"Ain't much," he said in a low voice, "a buck thirty-five. But I wanted you to have it in case you or Kate need something—like school stuff—that the old man won't pay for."

Halley tried to give it back. "You'll need it worse than us," she said. She looked over her shoulder at her grandfather. "Besides, I'm not sure Pa Franklin is going to let me go to school." She could have added that sometimes she wondered if she really wanted to do it badly enough. Her clothes would not be right. In this city school would probably be behind in all her subjects. How would she catch up and do all her work at home?

Gid shook his head and closed her hand around the money. "I don't need a thing. Ever'body says the CCC'll provide what I need. As for school, I already spoke to Kate and Ma. They both promised to speak up for you on school. You go, no matter what. It's your ticket out of here."

Gid squatted in front of Robbie. "You wave to Buck for me when you see him go by on the train, and you be a good boy when school commences." Standing, he turned to his parents.

"I'll write. Answer me back when you have a chance." He shook his father's hand and turned to his mother. Ma Franklin was crying into her apron.

Gid hugged her awkwardly. "No need to blubber, Ma. I'll be home for a visit 'fore you know it. They let CCC boys take leave ever so often. Let me know if that check don't get here and remember the first money out of it goes to hire out the washing. With Kate working, it'd just be you and Halley trying to do it."

Gid swung off down the road at a lope until he caught up with Buford. Ma Franklin broke into sobs and went back inside. Halley watched with Robbie and Pa Franklin until Gid disappeared.

||||||||||||||||||||||||||||||||||||||||||||||||||||||||||

8. Letters

HALLEY DID NOT GET TO GO TO SCHOOL. IT WAS HER GRAND-mother who sealed her fate. The old woman took to her bed with arthritis two days after Gid left.

So Halley was not surprised that night after supper when Pa Franklin said, "This does it. There's only the girl to keep the house going. There'll be no school for her until Ada is up and about."

Halley looked to her mother, hoping for another solution. School would be hard enough if she was there from the first day. To begin late made it just that much worse.

Kate kept her eyes downcast. "When Ma gets better, you can go," she said at last. "You can catch up."

Halley tried to make her mother understand. "Mama, this is not like the little country school I've been going to. This is a high school—in town."

Kate did not answer.

Halley turned to her grandfather. "Couldn't you look after Ma Franklin just during the day? I could put something on to cook before I leave in the morning and . . ."

"Cooking and taking care of sick folks is woman's work," said Pa Franklin. "Look in your Bible."

At that moment Halley hated them all—her grandfather who could cancel her entire future without a thought, her grandmother who had caused it all by just giving up and going to bed, and Kate, who was not willing to speak up for her.

Ma Franklin did not get better. Suddenly Halley was doing practically all the household work except for whatever help Kate could give after work and the little bit Robbie was willing to do. There was almost no time to tuft except at night, when she was so exhausted she often fell asleep after only a few minutes of stitching.

September moved on into October and with it cooler weather came. Pa Franklin did not hire anyone to help with the wash, so Halley began washing on Saturday, weather permitting, when Robbie would be home and Kate had a half day off from work. One Saturday in mid October she had the wash pot boiling and was slathering lye soap on her grandfather's work overalls.

"Put more wood around the wash pot," she told Robbie when he poured a sloshing bucket of water into the rinse tub. "The water needs to be boiling."

Robbie threw down the bucket. "I'm tired of working."

Halley felt like screaming at him. But she held herself back. He already got yelled at too often by Pa Franklin. "I'm tired, too, Robbie, but the washing has to be done, and until Mama gets home, there's only you and me to do it."

"Washing is woman's work," Robbie declared. "Pa Franklin said so. Boys don't do washing."

"They do when their big sisters need them," she told him. She did need his help. She wanted to see Bootsie at the church, and she needed to go to the Calvins' to drop off the latest spread she'd done, and pick up new ones. There would be money to pick up, too—fifty cents, unless Mr. Bonner had found a mistake. With that, she would have two dollars and fifty cents from tufting. She looked at the spread hanging over the back of her grandmother's rocker, just waiting for her to finish the wash.

Putting the overalls down on the big rock next to the wash pot, Halley picked up the batting stick and stirred the boiling towels. "Robbie," she said, "I'll let you beat the towels. You can hit harder than me."

Robbie grinned at the flattery. He always pretended the towels were enemy soldiers or wild animals coming at him.

Pa Franklin came out onto the front porch. "Girl, see to your grandmother," he said.

Halley took a deep breath. Why couldn't he wait on Ma Franklin, at least while Halley was doing the wash? Whether it was a drink of water or help with the chamber pot or bathing, he called Kate or Halley. He acted as if it would be a disgrace to see his wife's nakedness, but he surely must have seen it more than a few times since they'd had seven children together.

"Just a minute," she called to her grandfather. She fished out several steaming towels and splatted them down on the rock. "You can beat these while I'm gone," she said to Robbie, "but don't get near the wash pot."

Her grandfather was drawing a Jesus message on one of his crosses at the kitchen table when she walked in. His back was to the bed where his wife lay. After Ma Franklin had taken sick, she decided she wanted their bed moved into the kitchen where it was warmer. Two sheets hung on a wire strung from wall to wall provided a little privacy when needed.

For some reason, Pa Franklin had been reluctant to leave their bedroom, but he finally gave in. He still went to the bedroom at least once a day and usually stayed there a long time. Praying, Halley figured, but she didn't worry about it. The longer he stayed in there, the less she had to put up with him.

The smell of baking sweet potatoes and simmering beans filled the kitchen. Halley had put these on to cook right after breakfast. Her stomach growled. She was already hungry.

"I need my chamber pot," Ma Franklin said, raising up with a groan. The corn shucks in the mattress crackled under her shifting weight.

Halley pulled the chamber pot from under the bed and helped her grandmother slowly out of bed. The old lady's bones popped as she lowered herself to the pot.

Halley averted her eyes from her grandmother's exposed rear end. Surely she herself would never be this wrinkled and helpless. She would rather be dead.

"I'll change gowns so you can wash this un," Ma Franklin said.

Halley groaned inwardly. She had plainly asked her grandmother to change after breakfast, and she'd refused.

"My pillowcase, too. It's sour smelling."

"I changed it yesterday."

"It's sour again."

"Yes, ma'am," Halley answered politely, though she was irritated. She hurried to the chest at the foot of the bed. By the time she had the pillowcase changed, her grandmother was ready to be cleaned up and changed into her clean gown. The old lady had to be put back to bed, and then the chamber pot had to be emptied and washed.

Halley was sliding the pot back under the bed when Ma

Franklin said, "I'm sorry, child. I'm working you to death, and I'm not good for a thing in the world."

Shamed by her grandmother's meekness, Halley said, "You're good for some mighty fine stories." On Ma Franklin's good days she had told Halley stories of her young days.

Suddenly, Robbie screamed.

"What in tarnation!" Pa Franklin said.

Halley dashed across the room and through the dogtrot. Robbie was dancing around the yard, holding his right arm. "I was trying to get another towel," he said.

Halley rushed him to the tub of cold rinse water and plunged his arm in. She went weak with relief when she examined it a few minutes later. It wasn't blistered, only reddened. She dipped the arm again, fussing on him all the while.

"You ain't supposed to put a burn in cold water," Pa Franklin advised from the porch. "Warm water'd be better, they say. Then you rub butter or kerosene on it. Worse it hurts, the better for healing."

When Pa Franklin went back inside Halley said, "Robbie, why don't you go see if we have any mail." They had been getting frequent letters from Gid. He was over his homesickness now. He loved taking classes and playing games with fellow CCC boys. They had good food and plenty of it. On Saturdays, he could go to movies and sometimes to dances. It sounded like a good life.

When Robbie returned with letters, she didn't stop. She wanted everything washed, starched, and hung out to dry when she put dinner on the table.

She met her goal. When she emptied the washpot and tubs over the ashes of the fire, it was just a little past noon. After feeding her grandmother and helping her with the chamber pot once again, she sat down at last to the table with her grandfather and Robbie. Her legs were trembly.

Pa Franklin asked the blessing and slapped a letter down on the table backed in Gid's scrawled handwriting. "The usual partying and foolishness going on. If he lives to get out, Gid'll be ruint forever."

"Bet he's learning a lot," said Halley.

"Oh yeah," said Pa Franklin. "He's learning how to eat, drink, and make merry. Just like the Prodigal Son in the Bible when *he* went off to a far country."

"The Calvins say CCC's good training for a young man."

"The Calvins can afford to say all kinds of good things about CCC—they ain't got a boy in it."

Halley fell silent. She could hear Goliath thumping about on the porch and then the dogtrot and then the porch again. He was growling. Probably had caught a squirrel and was carrying it around like a prize, as he always did when he made a kill.

Pa Franklin pulled another letter from his shirt pocket and squinted at it. "From what the Woodall girl says, Alpha Springs has as many willful children as we have around here."

"Dimple?" Halley asked, looking at the letter in her grandfather's hand. It was Halley's letter and he had opened it! She wanted to rip it from his hands and run with it. He had no right to open her mail. No right to read what Dimple had written and talk about it as if it was *his* letter.

"Says some folks are saying Orrie Gravitt died of a broke heart. That boy-crazy daughter of hers, Lula May, told her she was getting married, and after that Miz Gravitt just give up."

Halley clenched her fists in her lap. Anger burned hot in her chest. Pinpricks of light seemed to explode in her brain. "I don't blame Lula May one bit," she said. "If she let them make a slave out of her, she'd never get a chance to have a life of her own."

"Sounds to me like you got a boyfriend in mind for yourself."

Halley blushed. Had Dimple teased her about a boyfriend in the letter? Surely not.

Pa Franklin slid the letter across the table, and Halley snatched it and wadded it into a small ball right in front of her grandfather's eyes. She had no interest in reading it now that he had ruined it. In this house Halley couldn't even have a letter to call her own. She was going to write Dimple that very night and tell her not to send any more letters to Pa Franklin's box. From now on her letters would go to Clarice.

Halley was no longer hungry, but she forced herself to finish the sweet potato on her plate.

Kate arrived as Halley was clearing the table. "What's Goliath dragging around the yard out there?" she asked.

"Oh no," Halley moaned. Surely Goliath hadn't pulled laundry off the line. That was puppy stuff. When Halley got to the porch, she screamed in anger and disbelief.

"My spread!" she yelled. Goliath had pulled her bedspread off the rocker and was dragging it through the dirt. She could see two big holes in it.

Furious, Halley took out after him, screaming to the top of her lungs. She scooped up rocks and pelted him. Goliath dropped the spread and headed for the woods.

Halley stayed right behind him, throwing everything she could get her hands on. "You sorry dog. I hate you."

Somewhere back behind her, she heard her mother and Pa Franklin call, but she paid no attention. Her only thought was revenge. Finally her foot caught in a vine and she pitched headlong into a briar patch. Halley didn't even try to get up. She simply curled up and cried about everything that had gone wrong in the last three months.

"You all right?" Kate asked when she arrived. She pulled Halley to her feet.

"No! I hate this place. I hate Pa Franklin, and I hate that dog. I'll have to pay for that spread out of money I saved for Daddy's gravestone. I worked so hard, and all for nothing."

"You left it where Goliath could get it."

"The wash is where he can get it, and he never bothers it. Grandma has left her shawl on that rocker lots of times and he doesn't get that."

Kate nodded. "There must've been some smell on that spread that got his attention."

"Yeah. *My* smell. He hates me."

"Maybe it's not a complete loss. If we can mend the holes, we'll use it on our bed."

"No! I never want to see it again."

Back at the house Goliath was on the porch hugged up against Pa Franklin's rocker. "Just blame yourself," the old man said. "You left temptation in the dog's path. Course you can blame your brother, too. He's been playing keep-away with Golly—training the dog to chew on stuff."

"I'm going to the church to clean," Halley said.

"Girl!" Ma Franklin called when Halley passed the door into the kitchen. "Come read the Bible to me." Halley had been doing that a lot lately. When she tired of reading, she could always ask the old lady for a story about her youth.

Halley opened the kitchen door. "No time to read now, Grandma," she called. "Got to go clean the church."

On the way to the church Halley took Dimple's letter from her pocket. Smoothing it out, she read it and then tore it into tiny pieces. Her anger swelled afresh as she sprinkled them in the ditch.

Bootsie was in the church when Halley arrived. She must've

come straight from the mill. Lint still clung to her red hair. She'd already begun sweeping the floor, but she stopped when she saw Halley's face.

"What's wrong?" she asked, setting her broom aside.

Halley told her everything.

Bootsie hugged Halley tight. "I'm so sorry," she said, sitting down on a bench and pulling Halley down beside her. "I wish I could help."

"How is everything with you?" Halley finally asked.

"Good as I can expect, I guess. Old Miz Duncan offered me money to keep quiet about ever'thing, and not to go to court. Said she'd see I keep my job till I start showing."

Halley was embarrassed for her. It was almost like getting paid for doing things with Stan. "Are you going to take the money?"

"I told her I'd think about it. But what else can I do? I can't make Stan do the right thing, or be the man I thought he was. And if he don't want me, he wouldn't give me anything but misery if he did marry me. Funny thing, Halley, Gid told me months ago he loved me and would marry me in a minute, but I was so stupid, I wouldn't give him the time of day. Now I can see Gid is worth a thousand of Stan, even if Gid is a skinny little runt without two dimes to rub together." She gave a bitter laugh. "Course, Gid wouldn't have me now."

"He's gone off to the CCC Camp," Halley said.

Bootsie nodded. "I heard your mama telling somebody at the mill right after he left, and then I started getting letters from him. I been trying to decide if I ought to write back. I wish I could tell him how I'd feel about him now, if I could go back and do things over, but . . ." Her voice trailed off.

Halley squirmed just to think about writing such a letter to a man. Bootsie's problems made her own seem small. Even the torn up bedspread and the opened letter seemed nothing in comparison.

"What are you going to do?" Halley asked.

"Well, I ain't going to kill my baby, which was Miz Duncan's main idea. She knows somebody in Dalton who can 'get rid of it,' she says. I told her, 'None of this is the baby's fault.' And then I told her, 'This might be the only grandbaby you'll have. You ever think about that?' Might be the only baby *I* ever have, and I ain't killing it."

Bootsie fell silent for a while and then she said, "I reckon I'll take whatever money Miz Duncan offers. I'm saving all I make at the mill, ever' penny except what I give my sister for board. I don't have to do nothing for now. If I'm lucky, it'll be maybe three months before I'll really be showing."

"How can you be so calm about it?" Halley asked. "You're not all torn up the way you were."

Bootsie smiled. "That's the best part, Halley. God saved me. And He told me He was going to take care of me. He told me that somehow everything is going to be all right. Ever since then I ain't had nothing to be anxious about."

Bootsie picked up her broom and began sweeping. The girl's face was more serene and happy than Halley had ever seen it. With all her heart, Halley hoped that everything *was* going to be all right.

9. Garnetta Pays a Visit

COLD WEATHER BROUGHT MORE TROUBLE. LOTTIE, THE MAIN milk cow, fell into a ravine and got killed. Buying a replacement took all of the first CCC check and more. "I talked Hewitt down on his price," Pa Franklin bragged when he led the new cow home. "Sukie's dropped two sets of twin calves already. She'll end up paying for herself."

They soon found out why Hewitt was willing to be talked down. Sukie was particular not only about which side she was milked on, but also about who could handle her. She favored men. She would kick and swing her horns every time Kate or Halley got near. To Halley's delight, Pa Franklin had to begin doing the milking night and morning, and it was about to kill him. "Milking is woman's work," he kept grumbling.

He grumbled louder when Sukie took to hiding at evening milking time. The other cow, Bessie, would come running just like Lottie always had, at the first rattle of the feed pail, but Sukie would lie down in tall grass or behind a clump of blackberry vines and be real still to keep her bell from ringing. The colder it got, the more often she hid.

Finally, Sukie started escaping from the pasture altogether and heading to Belton. One time the sheriff penned her up and charged Pa Franklin two dollars bail. Word got out, and neighbors began to talk and laugh about the Prodigal Cow. "Seen your cow yesterday, preacher," someone would say. "She was heading to town. Reckon she'll end up in jail again?"

Pa Franklin didn't take such teasing too well. Worse, he had to leave off painting his Jesus messages to repair fencing.

84 HALLEY

That was what he was doing on the last Saturday in October when Garnetta Miller came to visit at last, bringing Frank Earl and Dimple and lots of good food.

Robbie was overjoyed to see his friend. "Now you can go see my dog ride through on the two o'clock train," he said when he met Garnetta at her car. "Buck's a train dog now."

Halley felt shy. Both Dimple and Frank Earl had grown and changed in the two months since she'd last seen them. Dimple was growing a real bosom at last, and Frank Earl was showing a few sprigs of beard. Most important, they seemed interested in each other.

"I'll certainly have to go see that wonder dog," Garnetta said, handing a food basket to Robbie and a bigger one to Frank Earl. "Let's warm ourselves in the house before Frank Earl goes out to split wood."

Pa Franklin arrived as they all headed through the dogtrot to the kitchen.

"What you doing out there in the pasture, Webb?" Garnetta asked after they'd exchanged greetings. She suppressed a smile. "Looking for your cow again?"

Pa Franklin heaved a big sigh. "I take it you stopped at Shropshire's Store. I'm surprised they could take time off from deciding whether Roosevelt could win the election next month to catch you up on local gossip. Well, if'en the Old Woman can get well, I'll have the last laugh yet. Ada will break that cow from hiding and running around, and she'll milk it, too, or know the reason why. They ain't never been no cow that could conquer the Old Woman."

"Ma Franklin took to her bed a few weeks ago," Halley explained.

"I heard that, too," said Garnetta. She turned to Pa Franklin. "And they tell me you didn't send for a doctor yet?"

Robbie spoke up. "Miz Horn told Miz Bunch Sunday that she couldn't believe the preacher ain't sent for a doctor. And then Miz Bunch said he was going to let Grandma die."

Halley rejoiced in her grandfather's obvious discomfort. She'd been begging him to get a doctor for weeks, and even Kate had meekly suggested the same thing a time or two.

"If'n them old busybodies had been a praying as hard as they've been a gossiping, Ada might have been healed already," Pa Franklin said. "But for your information, I was aiming to get a doctor this coming week."

Halley's heart grew lighter at this commitment. Pa Franklin was big on keeping his word. Over the weeks of nursing her grandmother, of reading the Bible to the old lady, and listening to her stories, Halley had realized that Ma Franklin was a better woman than she'd given her credit for. Halley also had selfish reasons for wanting her grandmother well. The sooner Ma Franklin was up and about, the easier life would be for Halley. Though she felt it was too late to start school this year, she might at least have time for tufting more spreads and earning money.

"Is Miz Franklin going to die?" Dimple asked when they were back outside, finishing up the wash.

Halley hugged herself against a sudden cold breeze. "I don't know. I hope not."

Dimple sloshed a pair of overalls up and down in the tub of rinse water and then wrung them out. Finally, she spoke. "I tell you what I think: You better be looking out for yourself, Halley Owenby. I'd be picking me out somebody to marry if I was you. If that old woman dies, you ain't gonna be nothing but a slave around here. By the time all the old folks die, you'll be like my mother's old maid sister—too old and wrinkled to get anybody, or go to school, or anything else."

"I already *am* a slave," Halley admitted. "They're not letting me go to school. All that money I saved and the money from tufting, and I still can't get an education."

Dimple smiled. "That reminds me," she said, reaching into her pocket and pulling out a tobacco sack. She looked toward the woodpile where Frank Earl was chopping away, and dropped her voice to a whisper. "Your part of this year's ginseng money. Twenty dollars and fifty-two cents—not as much as when you're with us to find the best places. Me and Garnetta decided the three of us was a team and you still get your share, and we ain't going to have it no other way."

Halley shook her head. "I didn't help, so I didn't earn. Besides, I heard about your pa's mule. You'll need all you can get for a new one."

"I can't give Pa money without telling how I got it! Besides, the mule is nearly paid for. We had three calves to sell. Pa sold old man Henry them five acres with the spring that he'd been a wanting for twenty-five years, and then there's the money Pa's getting for working on the county road crew. They're finally fixing our road."

Halley put the tobacco sack in her pocket. "Thank you," she whispered. This money would bring her close to a hundred dollars. It was a fortune.

Frank Earl took time off from his job to help them empty the tubs of water when the girls had hung the last of the wash on the line.

"Pa and Uncle Clyde sold out the last run," Frank Earl confided to Halley, "and they still ain't making any new shine." He smiled proudly.

Halley nodded. She still didn't feel good about her uncles. It was aiding them that caused her father to get killed. Their refusal to help after Jim's death doomed Halley's hope of staying in her own home. But, she reminded herself, none of this was Frank Earl's fault.

Kate's arrival put an end to the conversation. While Kate spoke to Frank Earl and Dimple, Halley went to get the hair brush so she could get the lint out of Kate's hair. This was not an easy job. Kate's hair was thick with a bit of curl in it, and it fell below her waist. Kate always looked young and helpless with her hair down.

By the time Kate pulled her hair back into its usual bun, Garnetta was calling them to dinner. It was a feast. To the baked sweet potatoes and beans Halley had put on to cook that morning, Garnetta added fried pork chops and gravy, peach pickles, two cakes and two pies. Ma Franklin would not get out of bed, but she did eat a bit when Halley took some food to her.

After dinner, Garnetta announced that it was time to go to Crider's Switch to watch Buck ride by in the train. When they returned, Garnetta gathered up her dishes. "Time to head back to Alpha Springs," she said. "Got to allow time to change at least one flat tire. Glad I got Frank Earl along for jobs like that." She smiled at Pa Franklin, "Not that I couldn't do it myself, mind you!"

It was a lonely feeling for Halley, watching the car leave the yard. With all her heart she wanted to be in it, headed to her real home. At the same time she realized that it wouldn't be home anymore. Not without her father.

10. A Loss

NOVEMBER ARRIVED. TO NOBODY'S SURPRISE, PRESIDENT ROO-
sevelt was reelected. "Now let's see if he can do something
about the Depression this time round," said Pa Franklin.

November brought colder weather, too. Hog-killing
weather, Pa Franklin said several times, apparently hoping
to rouse his wife to make more effort at recovery.

As he had promised, on the Monday following Garnetta's
visit, Pa Franklin had fetched a Doctor Graham, an ill-tem-
pered man in a soiled suit and filthy shoes. He was known to
be the cheapest of local doctors. The medicine he'd left—a
powder to be measured on the tip of a pocket knife and taken
three times daily—had done no noticeable good. The two
elder Franklin daughters came, along with various neighbor
women, and brought remedies with no better results.

Finally, one bitter, cold morning when Halley was straining the fresh milk into a scalded jug, Ma Franklin called her.

Halley sighed, expecting another chamber pot errand. But
it wasn't. Ma Franklin motioned her close. "I ain't going to
git well if something ain't done." She paused for breath and
then continued, "Atter breakfast, when the Old Man heads
out to see Mr. Calvin and Mr. Walker about swapping out
work on hog killing . . ." She paused for breath again. "I want
you to fetch that Gowder girl, if'n she ain't already took off
to go to that school up north."

"Opal?" asked Halley.

Ma Franklin nodded. "Don't tell Old Man. He fusses ever'
time I take her remedies."

Halley returned to work. While Kate set out plates and forks, Halley took the strained milk into her grandparent's room. The one good thing about cold weather was that she didn't have to make the long trip to the spring twice a day. Until it was even colder, the unheated bedroom was good enough for keeping milk and butter. Later, when the temperature dropped well below freezing, they would have to use the cellar. She brushed the sand off the hearth and set the milk on the bricks.

On the way back to the kitchen Halley stopped to look at an old family photograph hanging on the wall next to the kitchen door. Obviously made when the Franklin children were still at home, it showed Kate younger than Halley. The baby Ma Franklin held on her lap had to be one of the babies that died. Maybe that baby was the lucky one, Halley thought.

Suddenly the door opened and Pa Franklin demanded, "And what you doing in here so long, girl?"

"I brought the milk in to stay cold, and now I'm looking at this picture," Halley answered.

"Use another room for the milk from now on," he said, "And you ain't got no call to look at nothing in my room."

Halley stalked by him back into the kitchen.

Soon they were gathered at the breakfast table. They were all bundled up in sweaters against the drafts of cold air. The flame of the kerosene lamp flickered with each breeze. The gravy and biscuits were already getting cold.

Kate quickly ate what little she had on her plate and gulped down her coffee, looking at the clock on the end of the table every minute or so. If she didn't get to the mill before the final whistle, the gate would be closed and she would lose a day's wage—maybe even her job. The biscuits and sweet potatoes she was taking for lunch were already in her lunch pail, waiting at the door along with the pail Robbie was taking to school.

Robbie was the only cheerful one at the table. "I bet the ice is froze solid on the pond," he said.

"You stay away from that pond," Halley said with a shiver.

"Ain't no danger if it's froze a foot thick," Robbie argued. She knew that most of his interest in the pond was pretend, intended to tease her, but then Halley never knew what foolish thing Robbie might do.

There was no help from Kate. It was as if she was somewhere else. As cold as it was, she had been up again last night praying until after Halley was asleep. When she finally got into bed, the coughing began and kept Halley awake. Kate's lungs had probably collected at least as much lint as her hair. She was coughing every night. This morning her eyes had dark circles under them. Then Kate was up from the table, pulling on her coat, mittens, and scarf. "See you tonight," she said to nobody in particular, and left.

Halley fed her grandmother and then pulled back the covers and helped her onto the chamber pot. It seemed that more came out of the old lady than went in. She ate less and less as the days passed. "We won't bathe today," said Halley. "It's too cold. I'll read to you after while and if you feel like it, you can tell me another story about when you were young."

Ma Franklin nodded. "First get Opal."

Robbie left for school, and soon after Pa Franklin took off in the wagon. Halley knew he'd not be back until after dinner.

Halley watched out the front window until her grandfather's wagon disappeared and then turned to her grandmother.

"I've let the fire burn low in the stove," she said, "and I've left you a glass of water here on the bedside table where you can reach it easy."

Her grandmother nodded.

"I won't be gone long."

Halley put on a second sweater and then her coat. She wrapped her wool scarf around her head and neck and then pulled on her mittens. Even so, once outside, she felt the wind to her bones. Puddles from the last sleety rain had a crust of thin ice over them. She could see where Robbie had stomped through several of these on his way to school.

As she left the yard behind, she looked toward the pond. The bare trees and bushes around it were like skeletons with raised arms. As Robbie had said, the pond was covered with ice.

A noise made her turn. Goliath had crept from beneath the house and was looking at her. The dog was keeping his distance from her since tearing up the spread. He was wise. Halley had not forgiven him. Every time she thought of the money she had to pay Mr. Bonner, she got angry all over again. Still, looking at Goliath now, on this cold day, and seeing him shiver, almost made her feel sorry for him. He was beginning to get that thin-hipped old-dog look about him. Probably he caught very few rabbits or other game now. If not for the handouts Robbie provided, he would probably starve. She pushed the thought away and ran toward the county road.

WITH ITS BARE TREES and windswept yard, the Gowder place looked as desolate as the Franklin place. Maybe more so, for the land was more sloping here, and washed-out gullies cut across the yard in several places. Columns of smoke rose from the chimneys of the two houses and one of the sheds. Beneath an oak was a large pile of broken pots.

Before Halley had time to wonder about this, the door of the shed with the smoking chimney opened and the girl named Opal came out and dashed two more pots against the pile. Shards flew everywhere. A dog barked in Halley's direction and then two more joined in. The last two were wagging their tails harder than they were barking.

"Opal," called a woman from inside the shed. "Two more pots."

"Yes'm, Mama Carrie," Opal said, her eyes on Halley.

"Why are you throwing your pots away?" Halley asked.

"Froze," Opal replied. "Froze and cracked 'fore we could fire 'em. They're no good."

A tall woman with chocolate skin stepped out of the shed. "Hush!" she said to the dogs, and they obeyed. She turned to Halley. "What you wants, child?"

"I'm Halley Owenby. My grandmother's sick. She wants to know if Opal can come."

Opal folded her arms and shook her head.

The old woman ignored the girl. "Who you grandma is?" she asked Halley.

"Ada Franklin."

The woman nodded and her face warmed. "Miz Franklin's ailing?" She motioned Halley inside. "What be wrong?"

In the shed, Halley drew close to the stove where pans of good-smelling food were simmering and told how her grandmother took to her bed weeks before, when Gid left. She told all the aches and pains she'd heard Ma Franklin mention. "And now she won't eat hardly anything. I'm afraid she's going to die."

"Mmmm-mmmm-mmmm," the woman said. She shook down the ashes in the stove and added several sticks of wood. "She will die if she doan eat."

"She need a *doctor*," said Opal. "Not me."

"She had one," said Halley. "He didn't help."

"Get another then."

Carrie silenced Opal with one look. "Miss Ada need more'n

a doctor can do. You take her some of my tea, and here's what you tell her . . ." She looked at Opal and Halley both. "You say it ain't her time yet. You say she have to eat. Then you say laying down to die is the easy road. You say she's got to take the hard road cause they's people that need her—chilren, grandchilren, her man. Preacher Franklin struts big, but he be lost without her."

Carrie handed a jar of herbs to Opal. "You go."

Opal went. Halley had trouble keeping up with her. At the county road she stopped and turned. "Preacher Franklin home?"

"No," Halley answered. "He'll be gone 'til late."

"Good," said Opal, and she took off again.

Goliath began barking when they reached the Franklin yard, but when he saw Halley pick up a stick he slunk back under the porch.

Inside, the kitchen was the same as when Halley left, except colder. Halley began to feed the fire at once.

Opal nodded approvingly. "Miz Franklin gone need a warm house so's she can set up in that rocker by the stove."

"Ma Franklin hasn't sat up in weeks," Halley said.

"Today she gone set up," said Opal. "She gone need something to eat. Something easy on her stomach. You gone need hot water for Mama Carrie's tea."

Opal headed back to the bed. While Halley emptied jars of homemade soup into a pot and set water on to boil, Opal talked in a low voice to Ma Franklin. To Halley's amazement the girl soon had the old lady out of the bed and in the rocker, bundled into a quilt, and taking soup and tea.

Pay, thought Halley. They would need to pay Opal something, and she was sure her grandmother had no money. Reluctantly, Halley went to the far room and took two quarters from her hoard. She got her tufting too and took it back to the kitchen.

Opal was still talking, saying all the things Carrie had said and acting as if the words were hers. Ma Franklin promised to sit up at least twice a day. "And like you say, I have to take the hard road. I know you're right. Thank you for coming."

Halley held out the quarters. "This is for you."

"I don't charge," said Opal.

Ma Franklin nodded. "Course you don't, cause you'd lose your gift. But I have to give you something or I don't get my cure." Ma Franklin acted as if she were paying—as if it was her own money.

Opal accepted the payment and left.

In the quiet that followed, Halley got her tufting and pulled her chair up next to the old woman. "Tell me about when you were young," said Halley.

"You don't want to hear all that," Ma Franklin answered.

"Yes, I do. And someday when I've got my education, I'm going to write books about how it was when my grandma was young a long time ago."

Ma Franklin looked at her, studying her face. "And you think people would want to read sich as that?"

Halley nodded. "You tell good stories."

Encouraged, Ma Franklin began a long tale about when she and Pa Franklin were young, "He was a softer man back then. Losing our first farm made him harder somehow. We used to go dancing."

Her eyes soon began to droop and then she fell asleep. Halley kept tufting. Except for eating a bowl of soup, feeding the fire, and one quick trip to the outdoor toilet, she tufted until her grandfather arrived home. She heard the wagon creak into the yard and on around the house toward the barn but did not get up. When he came in a short while later, he was surprised to find his wife out of bed.

"Didn't I tell you Doc Graham was a good doctor?" he bragged. "She'll be up and about in no time. Too bad it won't be in time to help with hog killing tomorrow."

His eyes fell on the tufting Halley was doing. So far he had ignored her work, and she had put off bringing up the subject. "You get paid for doing that?" he asked suddenly.

"Some. Not enough," Halley replied without looking at him. Her heart was pounding.

Pa Franklin kept looking at the spread, rubbing his chin thoughtfully, but, to her relief, when he spoke, it was on another subject. "Reckon I better set up the sawhorse tables for tomorrow's work," he said at last. Pa Franklin left and Halley began tufting with a new burst of energy. Maybe he was going to leave her alone this one time.

Robbie came home from school.

"Me and the Calvin boys went by Crider's Switch to see Buck's train," he said.

"Pa Franklin's going to hear you and fuss," said Halley. She could have pointed out that Crider's Switch was not on the way home, but well out of the way. She chose not to.

"Pa Franklin won't hear me. He went around the house toward the far room. I seen him when I walked up."

"Saw him," Halley corrected.

"Saw him. Anyway, the train was stopped on the sidetracks when we got there, and we got to talk to Buck and Tom Belcher too. Guess what? Mr. Belcher said he seen our cow next to Royster's Pond."

"Good heavens," said Ma Franklin. "She's out again!"

"No," said Robbie, grinning. "It was two days ago when he seen her."

Pa Franklin came in smiling a few minutes later, laying out his plans for the coming day. "'Course you'll have to have plenty of dinner cooked to feed them all," he said to Halley.

Halley groaned inwardly. She did well to cook for the family, without adding a group of working men.

Kate arrived home and wiped the smile off her father's face. "You're way early," he said. "Did you lose your job?"

"They had a lint fire," Kate said, holding her hands out to the stove. "They put it out before it did much harm, but they shut down so they could clean up." She looked at her mother. "You must be better."

"Lots better," Pa Franklin answered for her, "thanks to Doc Graham."

Halley didn't feel like hearing the praises of Doc Graham sung once more, so she picked up her tufting and headed for the far room.

As soon as she opened the door, something seemed wrong. The bed was rumpled, though she herself had made it this morning. Then there were the boxes with their underwear and night clothes. Instead of being neatly folded as usual, the clothing looked as if it had been stirred and jumbled. Perhaps Robbie had done it. But, no, he had come straight to the kitchen this afternoon, and she had been in the room earlier, to get the money for Opal. Everything had looked normal then.

Money!

Dropping to her knees, Halley jerked out the book box. The books were no longer stacked. They were jumbled helter-skelter. The cover of one was ripped loose at the spine, and another hung over the side of the box. Heart racing, Halley threw out books until she found her diary. The clasp was torn loose and the cover was open. It was empty. Her money was gone. It had been there that morning, and now it was gone.

Grabbing up the diary, Halley raced back to the kitchen. "My money!" she cried. "All I saved is gone."

"I needed it," Pa Franklin said. "Things like doctors don't come free. Barbed wire don't come free. And bags of curing salt ain't handed out for nothing."

"You took my money?" Anger filled Halley's chest. This was worse than anything he had done. Worse than reading her letters. Worse than making her miss school. "You stole my money."

"Halley!" Kate said, but Halley ignored her. She barely heard her.

"I didn't steal nothing, young lady," Pa Franklin said. "But what I'd like to know is how you come by that much money to begin with."

"Tufting and gathering ginseng with Garnetta Miller," Halley said, "and it's my money. Mine and Mama's and Robbie's. It wasn't yours, and we don't owe you anything. Mama pays you for our keep, and I work here every day."

"And you *still* owe me," he said.

Halley wanted to hit him. Instead, she lurched toward the front door, then stopped. "You'll not take any more money from me because I won't have any. I'll not tuft anymore. I'll not pick cotton. I'll not do anything for pay as long as I live in your house."

Throwing the door open, Halley ran outside into the freezing wind. Racing through the dogtrot, she almost fell over Goliath, who stood shivering next to the water shelf. The dog ran with her around the house, and when she opened the cellar door he darted down the stairs ahead of her. Only when she was huddled in a dark corner between the dog and a pile of sweet potatoes did Halley give way to tears.

11. Gid's Big News

When Halley returned to the kitchen near dark, Pa Franklin ordered her to continue tufting spreads. She ignored him. Later, in the far room Kate said, "Give in, Halley. We have to get along with Pa—and I've got to have some peace. Besides, the Bible says . . ."

"The Bible never said you had to let people walk all over you," Halley replied. "If *you* say I have to tuft, I'll do it, but nobody can make me do it right. And if I don't do it right, I don't get paid. If I keep doing it wrong, Mr. Bonner won't give me any more work, no matter what Pa Franklin says."

"Pa will punish you," Kate warned.

"What else can he do to me? I already work all the time. I wash, I iron, I cook, I clean, and I'm not allowed to go to school. He can't stand to see me read, and if he *allowed* it, I wouldn't have time. Now, on top of all else, he stole my money. What else can he do—kill me?"

Kate said no more. For the next few days the problem was delayed by hog killing. Even though several neighbors helped, there was still daylight-to-dark work for Halley. Kate helped each night when she got home from the mill. With instructions from Ma Franklin, who frequently sat in the rocker now, Halley fried the pork trimmings and strained the fat into lard cans. The cracklins left in the straining cloth, she put into jars to save for baking into cornbread and making soap.

Finally, on Friday, the last of the sausage was mixed and fried and packed in a crock and covered with grease. With Ma Franklin giving directions, the hog's head had been boiled and deboned, mixed with pepper, sage, and savory, and thickened with cornmeal and flour to make souse meat. It was packed into loaf pans and stored in the smokehouse along with the crock of sausage. The shoulders, middlings, and hams were out in the smokehouse too, packed in salt.

"We're fixed for meat," Ma Franklin said with satisfaction when it was all finished. "I appreciate all the hard work you done, Halley."

Halley was astonished, as much for the use of her name as the thanks.

Pa Franklin heard the comment but said nothing. That was fine with Halley. She neither expected or wanted thanks from him. All week while working with the meat Halley had thought of ways to escape. There was none except the solution suggested by Dimple—finding someone willing, and getting married. But even if there was a good match for her out there, how could she go off and leave Robbie? And, although she stayed angry with her mother a good bit of the time, she would feel guilty leaving Kate, too. To get married, she would need someone like Tom Belcher, Bootsie's new brother-in-law, someone willing to take on an entire family. Only an old man like Tom would be willing to do that.

Late in the day Halley was scrubbing the kitchen table to remove the last of the grease from the oilcloth when Robbie returned from searching for Sukie. His cheeks were red from the cold. "Found her and brought her to the barn," he said.

"Close the door, child," Ma Franklin told him, pulling her quilt closer.

"I seen Mama coming," Robbie said. Jamming a hand into his pocket, he produced a crumpled letter and handed it to his grandfather. "You got a letter."

Pa Franklin studied the envelope as if looking for a message on the outside. Halley tried to see it too, just in case Garnetta or Dimple had forgotten her instructions about sending any mail in care of Clarice.

Pa Franklin relieved her concerns. "About time Gid wrote."

Kate opened the door and a blast of cold wind came in with her. Lint flew from her clothing and her hair. Even after the long walk home in the wind she still needed brushing. Any anger Halley felt melted, at least temporarily, at the sight of her mother's thinness, which was obvious through all the layers of sweaters and coats. The anger was replaced with fear. What if something happened to Kate? Now that the money was gone, Halley and Robbie would have nothing saved. Whatever happened, they would be completely at Pa Franklin's mercy.

"We got a letter from Gid," Ma Franklin said to Kate. "Tell us what the boy says, Webb."

Unhurriedly, Pa Franklin slit the envelope with his pocket knife. "I can answer that ahead of time. He's going to tell about more foolishness." He drew out the letter and slowly unfolded it. Then he stopped and cleaned his glasses on his handkerchief. "Foolishment is the main thing they study in that CCC." He put on his glasses and waved the letter toward his wife. "Mark my words, Old Woman, the CCC'll be Gid's ruination."

Ma Franklin leaned forward, grasping the rocker arms with her vein-roped hands. "What does he *say*, Webb?"

Kate did not seem greatly interested. She went to the mantel, got the hair brush, and headed back toward the door.

Halley put out a hand, signaling *wait*.

Pa Franklin squinted at the letter and his face went red. "What?" he bellowed. "Gid's getting married! He can't do that. They'll throw him out and stop our check."

"Do we know the girl?" Ma Franklin asked.

Pa Franklin nodded. "We know her all right. It's the Hawkins girl. Bootsie." He said the name with distaste.

Halley felt a wave of relief that Bootsie would be married when the baby came. Then another thought came. Did Gid know about the baby? Surely not, but it really wasn't fair if he married Bootsie *not* knowing.

"Is Bootsie that girl that smokes cigarettes?" Robbie asked.

"Not any more," Kate said. "Bootsie says she's quit."

Pa Franklin grunted. "People can *claim* anything."

"I never see her with cigarettes at the mill these days."

Pa Franklin grunted again.

Ma Franklin sighed. "I was still hoping it'd be Clarice Calvin that Gid ended up with."

"That horse left the barn a good while back," Halley couldn't resist saying. "Clarice is keeping company with that feed and seed man. He gave her a ring, and Mrs. Calvin says it looks like a match."

"*Naturally,*" Pa Franklin said. "Gid'll let some other man run off with the best-fixed girl in the county while he hitches up with the very one he needs to run from." He sighed and read on. "He *thinks* he's gonna keep it a secret that they're married, so's he can stay in the CCC until he's able to get a job lined up somewheres."

"Nobody will hear it from me or my young'uns," Kate said and handed the brush to Halley. Still Halley hung back.

Pa Franklin threw the letter on the table and his wife reached for it. There was a long silence as she went through the pages, moving her lips silently as she read. At last, she folded the letter and took a deep breath. "Maybe it won't be so bad," she said to her husband in a meek and apologetic voice.

"Won't be so bad! How could it be worse?"

"Well, for one thing, the girl could be from way off somewheres else. With Bootsie being local, they likely will set up housekeeping hereabouts."

"They better not plan on moving in *here*," Pa Franklin said. "We got enough mouths to feed."

Ma Franklin ignored the remark. "Maybe we need to invite Bootsie to eat with us some Saturday or Sunday," she suggested as Kate handed Halley a coat and motioned toward the door. "I mean, now that she's going to be part of the family. If we treat her friendly like, she might not mind living close by."

Halley finally followed her mother outside.

For supper Kate and Halley fried the last of the fresh tenderloin. They had leftover baked potatoes, cabbage, and cornbread. Pa Franklin had just said the blessing and begun to pass the food when Goliath tuned up. Moments later there was a knock at the door.

"I'll get it," Kate said, and opened the door to the obviously pregnant Logan woman and three of her children. The smallest child was not much more than a baby, and it was propped on the woman's hip. The other two, Elmer, and a girl several years younger, carried lard buckets. All four were rail thin and poorly clothed for the weather. Elmer's eyes were on the floor and his face red.

Still, he spoke up. "That dog of your'n needs to be tied up," he said. "He's mean."

"Elmer's skeered of dogs," the Logan girl said.

"Shut up, Nellie," said Elmer, glaring at the child until she drew back against their mother.

"I ain't tying up my dog," Pa Franklin answered. "He's our protection. If you ain't doing nothing wrong, he won't do nothing to you."

"Come warm yourself by the stove," Kate said.

Ma Franklin squinted at the woman. "That you, Lillie Mae Logan?"

"Yes'm," the woman replied. "Hit's me." She moved over close to the stove. Halley couldn't help noticing that a great length of her hem was ripped out and hanging. The baby's face was crusted with food and dirt.

Elmer and his sister followed their mother to the stove. The eyes of the baby and the girl were on the table. Except for one quick glance at Halley, Elmer kept his eyes downcast.

"Lillie Mae," said Kate, "I went to school with you."

"Yes'm, a long time ago. I was a year behind you."

The woman looked older than Kate by at least ten years.

Kate looked at her father and then back to Lillie Mae. "We've just now sat down to eat." She hesitated, looked at her father again, and then rushed on, "We don't have that much, but you'd be welcome to share it."

"We wouldn't want to impose on nobody," Lillie Mae said. "'Sides, I got more young'uns at home needing to eat." She motioned to the lard buckets Elmer and his sister held. "I was just hoping I could borry corn meal and some beans. We ain't got nary bit of food in the house."

"That husband of yours off on a drunk again?" asked Pa Franklin.

The woman nodded with shame. Then a flash of defiance showed in her eyes. Elmer lifted his eyes and stared at Halley. There was defiance in his expression, too, and something more, a cold anger.

"I'm sorry as I can be," Pa Franklin said. "But times are hard, and I'm an old man. I got my ailing wife, my daughter, and these young'uns to take care of. I can't take food out of their mouths to feed the rest of the country. Your man ort to be taking care of his own."

"What did I tell you?" Elmer said and headed for the door. His mother was right behind him.

"Wait," said Robbie, jumping up. "You can have part of my supper."

"Mine, too," said Halley.

Without saying anything, Kate took the lard buckets from Elmer and his sister. Under her father's glowering stare, she took half the cornbread and meat off the table and put them into one bucket. In the other, she put half the potatoes. Ignoring her father's warning snorts, she scooped a number of cups of meal into one clean flour sack and several cups of dried beans into another.

"Thank you," the woman said.

Halley was full of pride in her mother. For once, Kate had done the right thing, despite her father.

Pa Franklin stood as Lillie Mae took hold of the door latch. "Wait," he said. "They's talk hereabouts on sending the Ku Klux Klan to punish that man of yours for neglecting his family. I ain't had a thing to do with it, but I hear talk. When Abner next sobers up, you might want to warn him."

"Daddy ain't afraid of no Ku Kluxers," Elmer said, throwing open the door. The wind blew in and the baby wailed.

"He'll be afraid when they're through with him," Pa Franklin called into the wind.

When Pa Franklin closed the door behind the Logans, he pulled the latchstring inside the room, and they all returned to the table. Ma and Pa Franklin had served their plates. There was one potato, two pieces of cornbread, and one piece of meat for Kate, Halley, and Robbie to divide. Besides that, there was only cabbage and buttermilk.

"Word'll be out after this," Pa Franklin said. "This'll be

the place to come for a handout. It's a mighty comfort to have a rich daughter."

Halley could tell by the way her mother was slumped in her chair that her burst of defiance was over. Kate spoke apologetically. "Pa, what kind of people would we be if we let little children go hungry?"

Halley spoke up with no remorse in her voice. "Jesus said if you do it for the least of these, you do it for me."

Robbie brightened. "You preached on that two Sundays ago, Pa Franklin!"

Pa Franklin's face reddened. "Don't you throw scripture at me! Charity begins at home. First feed your own, and if'n you have extry, *then* you help somebody that can't help themselves."

Nobody said anything.

"Ada can tell you what I'm talking about," he said, turning to his wife.

Ma Franklin did not rally to his support as she always had. In fact, she would not meet his eyes. She kept her gaze on her plate, which looked as if none of the food had been touched. "I can't help but recollect, Webb, how you told me that when you was growing up in that big family of yours, you allus had to leave the table still hungry."

"That's so, but here's the difference: we just went hungry. We never roamed the country begging food off other people's table. And we was always *clean*."

The meal was finished in silence. Halley looked at her empty plate and tried not to think of how hungry she still was, how much hungrier she would be before morning. Though it shamed her, *she* was also worried about how many more people might show up begging for food. Much as she hated to admit it, her grandfather was right about one thing—they couldn't feed all the hungry people in the mountains.

12. Bootsie Comes to Dinner

ONE NIGHT THE FOLLOWING WEEK, KATE ANNOUNCED THAT Bootsie was coming to eat dinner on Saturday. "She'll come home with me after work and spend the night. I'll put her and Halley in your room," she said to her parents. "They can share a pallet, and . . ."

"Not in *my* room, they can't!" said Pa Franklin. "They can sleep in one of the rooms across the dogtrot."

"Both the rooms over there need a lot more cleaning," Kate said, "so I thought . . ."

"You thought wrong. Nobody's using my room."

For a moment Kate looked angry, but then she mastered it and went on. "Bootsie said she'd help Halley clean the church on Saturday after dinner."

Pa Franklin was instantly alert. "And I wonder how come she knows about Halley cleaning the church on Saturdays?"

"Bootsie said she was there praying one day when Halley showed up to clean."

Pa Franklin snorted in disbelief. "*Her?* Praying?"

"That's right," Halley said. "Bootsie prays a lot."

"She *needs* to be praying," was all Pa Franklin said.

By Saturday at dinner, Halley had the wash done. The weather had warmed some, and so she used the hot sudsy water from the wash pot to scrub the kitchen and the room where she and Bootsie would sleep. Mr. Calvin had surprised them that morning with a big mess of beef from a cow he'd slaughtered, and Halley had put it in her grandmother's dutch oven to cook while she washed. Robbie had dug potatoes from the potato hill and brought them in, along with some overlooked carrots from the garden. They, too, were cooking.

"Golly found the carrots for us," Robbie said as Halley checked the pots of food on the stove.

Pa Franklin let out a rumble at the end of the table. "Goliath is a watch dog, not a pet. Sides that, I don't want him in the garden, lifting his leg on ever'thing growing."

Halley heard Bootsie's laughter outside. So did Pa Franklin. He frowned.

"Reckon they're here," he said. "I'll git a bellyful of that girl cackling today and tomorrow."

Robbie ran to look out the front window. "Bootsie is leading the cow! Sukie must've got out again."

"Tarnation!" said Pa Franklin. "I reckon I'm going to have to end up replacing ever bit of barbed wire around the whole pasture!"

"Sukie's following after Bootsie easy as you please," Robbie went on. "She ain't shaking her horns or nothing."

"Ain't it fitting that she'd be the only female that dumb animal would favor? Takes one to know one, I reckon."

Halley set the coffee pot on the hot part of the stove. They usually had coffee only for breakfast, but this was special. She was setting out plates when Kate and Bootsie walked in.

"We put your cow in the barn," Bootsie said. "She was headed to town. Old man Tyree loaned us a rope after he called that new dog of his off us."

"Blackie's a good dog!" Robbie said. "If you just squat down and let him sniff you, he'll get friendly."

"I'll remember that next time." Bootsie hugged Halley

and Robbie and then turned to the two old people. "Guess I'll soon be calling you Ma and Pa."

"That's what we hear," said Ma Franklin. She managed a quivery smile.

Pa Franklin had on his funeral face. "I'd as soon you keep right on calling me Mr. Franklin."

Bootsie kept smiling. "Whatever makes you happy."

"Something smells good," Kate said.

"It's a surprise," said Robbie, practically jumping up and down. "Want to know what it is?"

Bootsie rubbed his head. "You can whisper it to me."

Moments later Kate and Bootsie went outside to brush the lint off themselves. They'd left their coats inside. When Halley looked out the front window, she saw Bootsie brushing Kate's hair. With relief, she decided that Bootsie's waist looked as trim as it always had. The baby wasn't yet "showing."

Halley had the food on the table when Kate and Bootsie returned. "Mmm!" said Bootsie. "Anything that smells this good is bound to taste good. You can put money on it."

Pa Franklin glared. "We don't gamble in this house."

"Good," Bootsie answered smoothly. "I don't neither."

Pa Franklin asked a long blessing and then turned his eyes on Robbie and Halley. "Remember, we use manners in this house."

Halley knew this message was intended for Bootsie. If Bootsie figured this out, she didn't let it bother her. She kept up the happy chatter while the food was passed.

"Halley says you pray a lot, Bootsie," Ma Franklin said at the first pause.

"Yes ma'am," Bootsie answered. "I got saved a while back."

"Which church did you join?" Pa Franklin asked.

"None yet, but I go to church ever' Sunday. When Gid

gets a job, I'll join a church close to where we live. Me and the Lord ain't fully got that worked out yet."

Pa Franklin glowered. "Young woman, you need to do a lot more praying. When you really git saved, the Lord tells you what church he wants you in *right then*."

Halley tightened up, but Bootsie just smiled. "Maybe God does different ways with different folks, Mr. Franklin. The Lord tells *me* he's a lot more interested in whether or not I'm loving him and treating my neighbor like I want to be treated than he is in which church has my name on its roll. He just keeps telling me to trust and obey, and he'll show me the path. A month ago I wouldn't have believed I'd be marrying Gid. Now God's let me know Gid is the very man he intended me to have."

"Hhumph!" said Pa Franklin, but before he could say more, Kate spoke up.

"Has Gid got any word on a job outside the CCC yet?"

"Not yet," Bootsie said. "But you folks know more people around here than me. Do you know of any jobs?"

"They ain't none," Pa Franklin said. "Least ways, none that pay what CCC does. Jobs ain't that easy to come by."

Bootsie's optimism would not be crushed. "I'm not a bit worried. You forget, Mr. Franklin, this is in God's hands."

Ma Franklin let out a long sigh. "This is the first good meal I've tasted in a coon's age." Her plate was nearly empty.

"You want more?" Halley asked.

Ma Franklin shook her head. "I don't want to founder."

Pa Franklin pushed back from the table. He went to get his coat from its peg next to the door. "I have to go find where that blame cow got out this time, and fix the fence one more time."

Soon Halley and Bootsie headed to the church. Robbie

went with them. "I'll go play with the Calvin boys while you clean," he said when they were out of the yard. "Mr. Calvin got a goat and a cart for Dooley and Steve."

"You be careful, and you better get back to the church by the time we finish cleaning," Halley told him.

Robbie broke into a run. He was nearly out of sight when the girls got to the main road.

"You're doing better with Pa Franklin than I thought you would," Halley told Bootsie. "But I hope you don't have the thought that he's going to improve."

Bootsie laughed. "No, I was real sure he didn't like me before, and I figured he'd like me *less* as a daughter-in-law. But Miz Franklin seems like she's softening a little."

Halley agreed. "Being sick has changed her for the better."

"Well, they're both going to hate me when this baby comes a few months after me and Gid are married, and I just have to get used to that."

Bootsie was right, but Halley didn't say so. Instead, she asked, "Does Gid know about the baby?"

"He sure does. After I wrote him that me and Stan had broke up, he asked me to marry him again. I wrote back and told him I couldn't, that it wouldn't work now, and I told him why. He wrote back and said it didn't change any of his love for me and that he'd be proud to claim the baby if I'd let him. Can you believe that—he'd be *proud* to claim my baby! Oh, Halley, you can't know how much that meant to me. Gid is a good man."

Shortly before they reached the church, they heard a motor behind them and turned to see a car coming. It was Stan Duncan with a new girlfriend. The girl was behind the wheel, and the car was veering from one side of the road to the other. Both Stan and the girl were laughing. But Stan's laughter froze when he spotted Bootsie.

"I'm sorry," Halley said when the car rounded a curve and disappeared.

Bootsie shook her head. "Just save your pity for that poor girl Stan is fooling now. I just hope she's smarter than me—or, failing that, luckier."

The church cleaning didn't take long. To pass the time while they waited for Robbie, Bootsie played the piano and they sang. Finally, however, Halley realized how low the sun was getting.

"We better go get Robbie," she said.

They closed the church and headed out. The road circled the mountain and dropped sharply toward the bridge over Sipsy Creek. As the road dropped, the sun disappeared behind the mountain that sloped sharply up on the left. On the right, the downward slope was steep for about twenty feet and then it leveled into one of Mr. Calvin's fields.

They heard squeals of laughter up ahead, and then they saw the goat cart top the hill on the other side of the bridge. The goat was pulling the cart at top speed, and the two Calvin boys were chasing after it. Robbie was in the cart, Halley suddenly realized. Before that fully sank in, she saw a car top the hill behind the boys. Stan's car.

"Robbie!" Halley and Bootsie both screamed and began running to meet him. The Calvin boys leaped the ditch and climbed the road bank to get out of the way. The car honked its horn and the frightened goat put on more speed than ever and moved to the very middle of the road. At the last moment, the car swerved around the cart, one wheel in the ditch. It bounced over the bridge and headed straight for Bootsie and Halley.

Without even stopping to think, Halley shoved Bootsie

over the embankment and leapt down after her. Then she was tumbling over and over, hitting rocks and bushes in the way. Finally, she stopped and for a moment Halley was too stunned to move.

"Halley! Bootsie!" someone screamed above her. It was Robbie. Halley sat up and that's when she saw Bootsie a few feet away, lying in a crumpled heap.

"Bootsie," she whispered and crawled over to her. Bootsie was bleeding from several scrapes and scratches, and her coat was torn. Then she moaned and rolled over on her back.

"She ain't dead," said Robbie who had scrambled down the embankment in a shower of pebbles.

Bootsie's eyes opened. Her face was radiant, despite the scratches and bruises.

"You okay?" Halley said.

Bootsie nodded. "I'm fine."

Dooley crawled down the bank behind Robbie. "Is she alive?"

"More alive than I've ever been," Bootsie said. She sat up slowly, her face still turned skyward. Halley offered her a hand.

"We need to go toward the creek," Dooley said. "The bank ain't as steep there."

Slowly Bootsie stood, with one arm around Halley's shoulders. They made their way to the creek, where Bootsie scooped up handfuls of cold water and washed her face. When she stood, she grabbed her middle and doubled over.

"You okay?" Halley asked.

Bootsie gasped and then nodded. "I'm fine. You don't have to hold me no more. I can make it."

Halley climbed the bank to the road behind Dooley and Robbie. Steve waited there, holding the goat by its halter. "What's left of the cart is up there in the ditch," he said.

As she gained the road, Halley saw Stan and his girlfriend coming on foot. The car was slammed against a high road bank. Stan's door was gaping open.

"What do y'all mean?" Stan yelled, shaking a fist. "Blocking the road with a goat cart?" Steve backed away from him and dropped his hold on the goat harness. Stan kept yelling. "And you two gals in the middle of the road. You caused me to run my car into the bank and bend the fender."

"That's your fault, Stan," Halley said. "You're the one letting your girlfriend drive like a fool, and way too fast for a narrow mountain road. You could kill someone, and that's a sight worse than your car getting wrecked."

At that moment Bootsie pulled herself up on the road. Her red hair was a tumble of curls around her pale face. She looked from Stan to the girl for a long moment. Then she spoke to the girl. "You better take a good look at the company you're keeping. Stan never thinks about anybody but Stan. If you don't know that already, you're apt to learn it soon."

"You shut up," Stan yelled, his face blazing. "Come on, Linda," he said, wheeling around.

"I'm sorry about your cart," Halley said to Dooley.

Dooley shrugged. "Me and Steve can fix it."

"And our goat's okay," said Steve. "Do I need to go get Pa to give you a ride home in the truck?"

Bootsie smiled and shook her head. "It'd take more'n a little tumble to keep me down."

Without speaking they walked by the vehicle that Stan was trying to get out of the ditch. He raced the motor and spun the wheels to no avail.

Robbie sprinted for home, but Halley and Bootsie went slowly. Bootsie frequently took sharp breaths and grabbed her middle. They were passing the church when she stopped and whispered, "Halley, I'm going to lose my baby." She pointed to her legs. Blood ran down the insides of them.

Halley pulled her down on the road bank. Her mind was racing. Should she get Kate? No, Kate couldn't help and she might end up telling the Franklins. A doctor? Halley didn't know where the nearest doctor was. "Your mother," Halley said at last. "Do you want me to get Mrs. Hawkins?"

Bootsie shook her head. "She can't do nothing, and there's no sense in her knowing anything. I'll be all right in awhile."

Hurrying to the church, Halley got several of the clean dusting cloths. With them, she managed to clean Bootsie's legs and shoes.

"My coat hides my dress," Bootsie said at last. She stood. "I think I can go on now."

They went on even more slowly than before. When they took the turn to the Franklins, Halley asked, "Are you still going to marry Gid?"

"You can count on it. I got me a good, decent man that loves me, and I aim to keep him 'til death us do part."

Kate came out on the porch as they neared the house. Robbie and Pa Franklin were right behind her. "Robbie told us what happened. Are you all right?" she asked.

"A few bruises," Bootsie answered.

"And her period started," Halley whispered. "Mama, could you bring some water to the far room?"

Soon Bootsie was cleaned up and lying in the bed where Halley and Kate usually slept. Halley sat by the bed, thinking she was asleep. But then Bootsie's eyes opened.

"Something happened back there, when I fell to the bottom of that bank that I didn't tell you," she said. "When I rolled over and looked at the sky, there was a voice."

"A voice?" Halley asked.

"Sorta like in my head. I been called—called to preach."

13. Bud Gravitt's Gift

DECEMBER CAME, AND WITH IT BITTERLY COLD WEATHER. AT night when the fire died down in the stove, the temperature dropped below freezing. Ice formed on top of the water bucket before morning.

Kate never missed a day of work, not even the day it sleeted on top of a snow, not even the day following that when huge limbs were snapping off trees under the weight and crashing to the ground with sounds like thunder.

Robbie did miss a few days of school, and Halley had finally accepted that it was absolutely too late for her to attend school this year, even if her grandmother were suddenly well. Recovery didn't seem likely. Though Ma Franklin was out of bed most of every day, she went no further than the rocker next to the stove. The old woman was still unable to help cook, clean, or wash, and Halley wondered if she would ever be strong again.

Often the days were too cold to do the wash outside, and Halley had to boil the clothes on the stove and beat and scrub them on the kitchen table. Her grandfather hated the noise and mess of these days, but not enough to hire the wash done.

One day when Halley went to the far room to get a clean apron, she caught him going through her book box.

"I don't have any more money," she told him in a cold voice. Actually, she did have the very last money she'd earned on her tufting. Clarice had slipped it to her on one of the rare Sundays that Halley was able to go to church. That seventy-five cents was safely tied in her bosom, and it was going to stay there. Halley reached for a clean apron on the apron peg. "Pa Franklin, you already took everything I had, remember?"

"You mighty right, I took it," he answered without any shame whatsoever. "You eat here. You can help pay for the food. You can just go over to the Calvins tomorrow and tell them you're signing up for new spreads to tuft."

Halley jerked the apron over her head. She was as angry as he was, but she wasn't going to show it. "I'll be happy to tuft if you want to take over cooking, washing, ironing, churning, and cleaning the house—or hire someone to do it." Turning, she went out the door and headed for the kitchen. Pa Franklin was right on her heels.

"Set up at night and work like you used to," he said as Halley threw open the kitchen door.

"Kerosene for the lamp costs money, and you already said we had to cut back on that. Besides, I can't stay up every night *and* get up before daylight every morning. But *you* could start tufting. You could do it in the daytime instead of painting Jesus messages."

"Me?" he thundered. "You're talking about *me* doing spreads?"

"Webb," Ma Franklin said from her rocker. "Webb!"

He ignored his wife. "Girl, don't you get smart with me. I'm not doing woman's work."

Halley was ready for that argument. "Mr. Bonner says there are men all over these mountains helping their wives tuft because it's the only way they have of getting cash money.

You have lots of free time. I'll get some spreads for you, and I'll show you how to do the work."

"Nobody would have to know but us, Webb," said Ma Franklin.

"Ada!" he said. "I can't believe you've turned on me."

"I've not turned," she replied. "I'm just trying to help you get some more money, so you won't load more on this child."

Pa Franklin swung around and headed out the door.

A gloating happiness filled Halley's chest for a short while, but by the time she had started supper, she realized that her grandfather would only take out his anger on the others. He was harder than ever on Robbie. Several days before he had given him a whipping for sneaking a piece of cornbread out to Goliath.

"How many times have I told you not to waste food?" Pa Franklin had said, reaching for the switch beside the stove.

"Golly's hungry," said Robbie. "You can see how bony he is."

"Then let 'im go catch his own food, 'stead of begging," said Pa Franklin, bringing the switch down on Robbie's legs. "The dog'll have to get his own food at this house."

After this, Halley redoubled her efforts to keep Robbie busy after school. She thought up errands to the Calvin's or sent him to Carrie Gowder's to get more tea. When she could think of no errands, she tried to keep him out of Pa Franklin's sight. "Gather twigs for starting fires," she'd say, or "Check the barn to see if the chickens laid any eggs there."

That was what he was doing one Saturday when Kate got home earlier than usual. She changed into a clean dress and then returned to the kitchen with her hair let down so Halley could get the lint out. "Some of the machines broke down," she said when her father questioned her early arrival.

"Looks like all the easy money's about to end," Pa Franklin

said. "That whole place is about to close down."

Kate made no answer. "Come out on the porch and brush my hair," she said to Halley, handing her the hairbrush. "I need to get it back up."

The day was warmer than it had been in over a week, and there was no wind. On the far end of the porch where the sun was shining, it was almost pleasant. They headed for that patch of sunshine, where Goliath had already staked his claim.

"Move," Halley told him. Stiffly, he pulled himself to his feet and moved just enough to make room for them.

Halley began to brush. Kate's hair fell below her waist, thick and heavy. It gleamed in the sunlight, making Halley think of summer days when she had brushed her mother's freshly washed hair on their front porch in Alpha Springs. For a moment she pretended they were back in those happy days. Daddy was out in the barn cleaning a stable, and Robbie was trying to help. Mama would soon go in and start supper, and, as for Halley, she could read a book or work on her embroidery this afternoon. Or she might sit down to the piano one more time and try to coax out the music Robbie and her father always found there.

The illusion was shattered when Goliath suddenly leapt up and began barking. A truck loaded with furniture had turned into their road. There were two men in the cab. Robbie came running from the barn. The truck stopped, and Bud Gravitt stepped out in his going-to-town clothes. Halley had rarely seen him in anything other than overalls.

"Hey there, Robbie," Bud said, and then turned toward the porch and removed his hat. "Well, hello, Kate," he said, and then couldn't seem to remember what else he'd planned to say. He gazed at her for a long moment before finally saying, "You look good."

Blushing, Kate swept back her hair and tried to get it up in its usual bun, but it was no use—her hairpins were still in the kitchen.

"You look in good health, I meant to say," Bud said, "And you too, Halley." His eyes were still on Kate. The passenger got out of the truck, and Halley realized that it was the oldest Gravitt boy, the one they called Chub. The name must've been a carryover from babyhood, for there was nothing chubby about him now. He was tall, sturdy, and muscular, like his father.

"Hey," Chub said.

"We heard about Orrie," Kate said as Bud approached the porch. "I was mighty sorry. She was a good woman."

Bud twisted his hat brim in his hands. "Losing a mate is a grievous thing, as you yourself know."

"Yes, it's hard but a person has to go on."

Bud nodded. "But my baby boy is a fine 'un. Named him Will."

Kate smiled and closed her eyes. "Will," she said in a soft voice. "That's the name I picked for one of the babies I lost. I wish I could see *your* Will."

Pa Franklin came through the dogtrot hall and out onto the porch. "Howdy," he said somewhat reluctantly, Halley thought. He must be worried that the Gravitts would stay for a meal. "Come on in and warm up," he said.

"We don't have time to visit," Bud said. "My daughter Lula May got married and moved not far from here."

"We got word of that," said Pa Franklin.

"Well, I'm taking her a few furnishings, and while I was over this way, I decided to bring Kate something I wanted her to have." He motioned to his son, and Chub pulled a quilt off the biggest thing in the back of the truck.

Robbie's face lit up. "My piano!" he cried.

"Never felt right about buying it to begin with," Bud said. "Now, with Orrie gone, nobody at my house cares anything about it. Reckon music is one of them things you either got a gift for or you ain't."

Kate was shaking her head before he even finished speaking. "I can't pay you, Bud, and I won't allow you to give it to us."

"That's right," said Pa Franklin. "We don't need no piano. We got enough noise around here, way it is."

Halley, who had been wavering between a longing to reclaim this part of their old life and a reluctance to accept such a gift from the Gravitts, made up her mind. "Mama, let's take it."

"It'd be my pleasure if you'd accept," said Bud, "for the children."

Finally Kate nodded. "Thank you, Bud."

Pa Franklin let out an exasperated grunt.

Bud backed the truck up to the porch, and, despite Pa Franklin's grumbling, they wrestled it off the truck, across the porch, and into the kitchen. Robbie followed with the stool. By moving the cupboard a few feet in one direction and the flour and meal bins in the other, they had room to set it against the wall opposite Ma and Pa Franklin's bed.

Bud Gravitt took time to speak to Ma Franklin and tell her how fine she was looking. "It's easy to see where Kate gets her looks. I hear you've been ailing, but I bet you're well in no time."

Meanwhile, Pa Franklin kept muttering about how the piano crowded the kitchen.

"We'll move it to the far room come spring," Kate promised.

Robbie sat down to the keyboard but Halley stopped him. "Not now," she said. "We'll have to figure out when you can play without bothering anybody."

"That'll take big figuring," said Pa Franklin.

Ma Franklin reached a hand out to her husband as though to soothe him. "It might be nice to hear some good gospel tunes right here in our house," she ventured. "It's been so long since I could go to church and hear any. Reckon you could play, 'Beulah Land,' Robbie?"

"You hum the tune and I can play it," he replied, hugging his grandmother. "I can play anything."

Kate turned to Bud. "You and Chub have a seat while I go get my hair up."

Halley went with her mother to the far room and helped to put up her hair. Kate gave herself a long appraising look in the mirror as she tied on her best apron. Then, using her hands like combs, she loosened her hair a bit on either side. In the mirror, she caught Halley's eyes and blushed. "It felt tight," she said.

When they got back to the kitchen, the men were talking crops and weather. They discovered they both planted by the zodiac. "It's the only way to farm," said Pa Franklin.

"I just don't believe in taking chances myself," Bud Gravitt said. "I figure if good farmers been doing this way hundreds of years, there must be *something* to it."

"Well, I got a better reason," said Pa Franklin. "It's according to the Bible. You read Ecclesiastes where it says there's a season for ever'thing. A time to plant and a time to pluck up what is planted."

As if that was a signal, Bud Gravitt stood. "I reckon it's time I was going," he said.

"I was aiming for you to stay for supper," Kate said without any apologetic glance for her father.

Halley was astonished at her mother's boldness.

Bud looked sorrowful. "Me and Chub have to get that stuff over to Lula May's and then head on back home. Maybe I could take you up on that offer next time I'm over this way?"

Again, Kate spoke without seeking permission from her father. "You'd be welcome any time, Bud."

Halley noticed that her grandfather did not join in this invitation. But Bud Gravitt seemed unaware.

"Maybe some Sunday," he said. "I could hear Brother Franklin preach in his own church."

"He won't sound any better than he did in Alpha Springs," said Robbie, and everybody except Pa Franklin laughed.

Kate followed Bud out to the porch. Halley watched them from the front window. Kate kept smiling and patting her hair. Halley suddenly realized that not one time during the visit had she seen Kate hugging herself. Her shoulders were squared. She looked several inches taller than usual.

Halley turned back to the piano. It did feel good to have it back, although Robbie would only be able to play it when his grandfather was away. But when would she have time to try to learn to play? Bud Gravitt's words about either having a gift or not having it flashed across her mind, but she quickly dismissed them. What did he know about music? Besides, she had to believe that *something* good could happen in her life. After four terrible months where nothing had gone right, surely something would finally go the way she wanted.

14. A Trip to Belton

BUD GRAVITT DID NOT COME THE FOLLOWING SUNDAY. ALMOST continuous rains for three days had made the roads such a mess by Saturday that horses and wagons were having trouble using them. For trucks and cars, the roads were almost impassable.

"Shows how much Bud Gravitt's word is worth," commented Pa Franklin with satisfaction at Sunday supper. "He lets a little rain and mud stop 'im."

Kate said nothing.

Several days later a letter arrived from Bud Gravitt. Luckily, Halley was the one who went to the mailbox that day. She gave the letter to her mother when she went outside to brush the lint out of Kate's hair. Kate slipped the letter into her pocket without comment, but Halley caught her reading it after supper.

"Well? What about the letter?" Halley said when they went to the far room at bedtime.

"Robbie, go to the toilet before you put on your night shirt," Kate said. She was deliberately ignoring the question.

Halley jerked off her dress. "What did Bud Gravitt say?" she asked.

Kate tugged her dress over her head and pulled on her gown. "Grown women don't usually feel obliged to answer a daughter's questions about private things," she said, "but I'll tell you Bud couldn't make it this Sunday because of rain."

"I knew *that*. I'd like to know why is he coming to begin with?" Halley asked. "He gave us the piano. So why's he coming *back*?"

"I guess he's lonely."

Halley pulled on her flannel gown and unlaced her shoes. "His handwriting is awful."

Kate's teeth were chattering in the cold of the room. "Most men don't write a good hand."

Halley dived under the covers on her side of the bed. The springs rattled, and the rough sheets seemed to have ice on them. "*Daddy* had beautiful handwriting and good spelling. I noticed Bud Gravitt misspelled 'Alpha' in his return address. He can't even spell where he lives."

"Bud didn't have a chance to go very far in school," Kate said. "That's no sign he's not smart. Don't put yourself above him. I grant you he's not as educated or handsome as your father, but he's a good man—a man who takes care of his family."

At that moment Robbie burst in with a blast of cold air and so Halley had to hold back all the other things she wanted to say. Unfortunately, the temperature was dropping and roads were freezing. That meant cars and trucks would soon be able to move again.

The next morning Kate pulled Halley aside before leaving for work and slipped something into her pocket. "A tracing of Robbie's foot and my wedding ring," she whispered.

"What . . ." Halley began, but Kate shushed her.

"Go to Shropshire's Store," she said. "I don't have enough time off at dinner to do it myself, and after work, I have to hurry to beat dark. Talk to Tate Shropshire. Tell him I need to sell my ring to get Christmas presents for Robbie. Buy some rubber boots and a little candy. Maybe some kind of toy, if any money is left."

"Mama, your ring . . ." Halley began.

"Christmas for Robbie is more important. He's little. I wish I could get something for you, too, but I doubt Tate will give you enough money for more."

Halley shook her head. What she wanted, money couldn't buy.

"What y'all plotting over there?" asked Pa Franklin from the table.

"Halley's going to the store today," Kate said, hurrying to the table and sitting down. "You'll need to give her money for coffee."

"What? The coffee's gone already?" Pa Franklin said, but before he could say more, Robbie overturned his milk.

In his fury, Pa Franklin forgot all else. "You careless young'un! Do you think milk comes free?"

Ma Franklin grabbed a dish towel and mopped up the spill before it could run off onto the floor. "The child didn't do it a purpose, Webb," she said.

Pa Franklin turned on her. "Woman, you keep out of this. The road to hell is crowded with people who didn't do a single thing on purpose. The boy's going to have to learn to think what he's doing, and I guess I got to help him learn."

"My Lord, Pa!" said Kate, leaping up and putting her arm around Robbie. "A child going to hell because of spilt milk?" To Robbie, she said, "Get ready for school." She handed him two biscuits. "Go to the Calvins and wait there until Steve and Dooley are ready to go."

The Calvins were way out of the way, but Halley didn't point this out. She wanted him away from his grandfather's wrath as much as Kate did.

When Robbie was gone, Kate turned to her father. "Pa, I'm trying my best to go by the Bible and honor and obey you. But Robbie is my son and I owe him something, too. I'm asking you—begging you—to stop expecting him to be perfect. He's a child, and children make mistakes."

"And I ain't allowed to correct him?"

Halley was expecting the usual surrender. But to her surprise, Kate didn't back down this time.

"You know that's not how it is," she said. "I've kept quiet through several hard whippings. But you have to be fair."

Pa Franklin drew himself to his full height. "Proverbs 22:6, train up a child in the way he should go. Bring up a child in the admonition of the Lord."

Halley could keep quiet no longer. "Doesn't the Bible say something about not provoking your children? And it says, when I was a child I spake as a child."

"Well, you can see for yourselves what sparing the rod does," Pa Franklin said, waving his hand at Halley. "The girl's been allowed to plain-out tell us she won't work no more, and she got away with that. Now she's quoting scripture at us, just like that floozy Gid's about to marry. Now Bootsie's telling folks she's been called to preach!"

"Maybe she *has* been called." Kate shoved her chair up against the table. "I'm beginning to think Bootsie is better acquainted with God than a whole lot of preachers." Kate grabbed her coat, pulled it on, and picked up her lunch pail. She was out of the door and gone before Pa Franklin could reply.

After breakfast while Halley cleaned up, put beans on to boil and put sweet potatoes in the oven, her grandfather ranted and raved about how badly he was mistreated. Ma Franklin tried to soothe him but to no avail. By the time Halley gave her grandmother her cup of tea, Pa Franklin had pulled out Gid's letters and started complaining about him.

"Taking classes! Learning electric wiring! Fixing motors!" How's any of that going to be worth a hill of beans to him or us?"

"I've been studying on that," Ma Franklin said. "You recollect Gid didn't want to quit school back yonder when we
told him he had to."

"It don't matter what Gid wanted," said Pa Franklin. "We
needed help on this place to make a living!"

"I ain't blaming you," Ma Franklin said quickly. "You and
me both said he had enough schooling and we thought at the
time we was doing the best. But I still recollect how bad he
wanted to go when that woman come around trying to take
young'uns off to her school over yonder in Rome. High school
and college, she said, and he could work out what it cost."

Pa Franklin said, "You talking about that Martha Berry
woman with her big fancy school for mountain young'uns?
Well, I wasn't about to let that rich old maid take my boy off
to live at her school!"

Ma Franklin nodded. "I said the same at the time. But
maybe we was wrong, Webb. Miss Berry said she could train
Gid to be a better farmer if we'd let 'im go. Maybe he'd a took
more interest in this place if'n he'd went. Maybe he wouldn't
be wanting to leave now."

"Is that school still in business?" asked Halley, trying to
keep the eagerness out of her voice.

"This talk don't concern you, gal," said Pa Franklin. He
turned back to his wife. "Gid ain't never going to farm. School
or no school. He's going to git married and slave away his life
at some mill, like Ralph."

"If working at the mill is slavery for Ralph and Gid, why
is it okay for Mama?" Halley asked.

"Because Kate ain't worth nothing here on the farm, just
like you ain't worth nothing. Now, Gid and Ralph was good
workers when they tried."

The words hit Halley like a slap. She was worth nothing

and Kate was worth nothing. Halley tuned out the rest of the conversation. She got her coat, scarf, and mittens as if nothing had changed. In reality, everything had changed. She had just seen a crack in a closed and bolted door, and there was daylight beyond that door. Somehow she was going to go to that school that Gid had wanted to go to.

Halley spoke to her grandfather without her usual caution. "Do you want coffee or don't you? I don't care either way, but I'll need money, if you want it." Turning to her grandmother, she asked boldly, "Do you need anything?"

Ma Franklin shook her head. Pa Franklin stared hard at Halley, as if seeing the change that taken place in the last few minutes and trying to figure it out. "My, ain't we got bossy?"

Halley shrugged and looked at her grandfather until he averted his eyes.

"You and your Mama act like I'm made o' money," he said. Standing, he dug into his pocket and handed Halley two dollars and some coins. "Now you bring back ever' penny of my change."

Halley ignored him and turned to her grandmother. "You think you can manage the churning?"

Ma Franklin nodded. "I done it yesterday, didn't I? Carrie's tea is fixing me up." She was no longer bothering to keep the home remedy a secret.

Pa Franklin grunted. "I think it's more Doc Graham's medicine than that old bat's herbs."

Halley ignored him. "I got the churn close to the stove so the milk ought to be sour enough."

Ma Franklin nodded.

Halley went out to draw a fresh bucket of water. The winter sun had brightened the yard a little, and Goliath was curled up on the sunny side of the oak near the wood shed.

The dog looked so thin.

"You'll need to stir the beans every now and then," she said to her grandfather when she returned with the water. Thinking of Goliath, she scooped two biscuits from the warming oven and put them in her pocket. "The kettle has hot water in it, if the beans get too dry," she went on, ignoring her grandfather's scowl.

"You better help the Old Woman with the chamber pot 'fore you take off loafering," said Pa Franklin.

"No need," said Ma Franklin. "I'll manage."

"You sure?" Halley asked.

Ma Franklin nodded.

Moments later Halley was outside. It felt like being released from prison. She tossed the biscuits to Golly and then looked back at the front window. There stood Pa Franklin watching her. She looked straight back and lifted her chin. "I'm not going to be here long," she muttered. "I can stand anything for a little while."

At last Pa Franklin turned away, and Halley set out for Belton by way of the trail her mother used every day. It followed their pasture fence for a good distance and then it left Franklin property. From what Gid and Pa Franklin said, it went over the MacAfee land and skirted the edge of the two hundred-acre Tyree place before reaching the outskirts of Belton. Though she had never taken the path before, she wasn't worried about getting lost. There were side trails here and there, but the main path was well-beaten and easy to follow.

Hope bubbled up inside her like a spring. She was going to write Miss Berry in Rome, Georgia, this very afternoon. She would tell the woman that she was Gid's niece and that she wanted to go to school more than anything.

But the old worry came—what would happen to Robbie?

She argued with herself that Kate was beginning to stand up to Pa Franklin. She had not allowed him to whip Robbie this morning. But on the other hand, Kate was gone a good bit of the time. And what about after school? What about Saturday mornings?

But what about me? she thought. What about my life and what I want? And like Clarice said, how was Robbie going to learn to take care of himself if *Halley* kept doing it? Nobody had ever looked after Halley that way. She'd had to learn to take care of her own problems.

Halley's pace grew slower and slower as she debated back and forth. Suddenly her eyes caught a movement across the field. A dog. It had to be Mr. Tyree's dog, Blackie. Despite what Robbie had said about the dog, she wanted to keep her distance. "Just don't never run from it," Robbie had said. "And don't look 'im straight in the eye."

Quickly averting her eyes, Halley made sure to keep her pace slow. The trail began to drop and soon the dog was out of sight. Gradually she became aware that she was smelling smoke. Not, she thought, from anyone's chimney. The MacAfee house was probably closest and it was far back behind her. This smoke was much nearer. As she looked about, she spotted it—a trail of smoke rising from a little wooded ravine down to her left. Was it a forest fire? Unlikely, since the ground was so soaked from recent rains, but if so, she would need to tell someone.

Leaving the trail, Halley crept downhill, circling around clumps of underbrush. Just ahead was the ravine, and that's where the fire was. Then she was at the edge and, looking down, saw a man or a tall boy squatting with his back toward her. In front of him was a pile of burning boards. White boards and crosses, she suddenly realized, with lettering on them.

Jesus messages! She sucked in her breath sharply and backed up, and as she did so, a shower of pebbles and debris broke loose under her foot and cascaded downward.

"Hey!" a voice yelled. "Stop!"

Halley ran uphill toward the trail. Behind her she could hear someone scrambling up the bank of the ravine. Just as she reached the trail, a hand grabbed her shoulder and swung her around to face—Elmer Logan.

"What you mean, spying on me?" he asked so close to her face that she could smell his foul breath.

"I wasn't spying," she said. "I—I thought the woods had caught fire."

"Likely story, wet as it is!" Now he had her by both shoulders, and his fingers were squeezing through the layers of her sweater and coat into her flesh. "You seen what I was burning."

Halley tried to think of a lie he would believe, but couldn't. Finally she nodded.

"The Jesus man s'posed to be a preacher, but he treats me and my family like dirt. Well, I'm getting even. You ort to be helping me. He treats you like dirt, too."

Halley shook her head.

"I'm burning on Tyree land, which is fitting—Old Man Tyree ain't treated us much better than the Jesus man. Nobody'll ever know it was you and me done it."

"No."

"Oh no, not miss good-goody. She wouldn't dare do nothing wrong. Now I guess you're going to tell on me."

"If you stop, I won't," Halley promised. "If you don't take any more of his signs, I'll keep your secret."

Elmer pushed her up against a tree. His knee shoved between her legs. "Miss Halley Owenby," he whispered. "Thinks she's too good to walk to the spring with me. Laughed at me for asking."

"No, I didn't. Some of the other girls laughed, but I didn't. And it wasn't you, I swear. I didn't walk with *anybody*."

"See if I'm good enough for this," he said and thrust himself up against her. Then his mouth was on hers.

Halley flung her head from one side to the other. "Stop!" she screamed. "Stop."

"Scream all you like, and I'll do whatever I want. Your great big dog ain't here to pertect you now."

"Mr. Tyree's dog is. He's right up the trail. He'll come, and he'll kill you. Blackie!" she screamed. "Blackie! Come!"

"Hush!" Elmer put one big hand over her mouth and knocked her head against the tree so hard she saw stars. "Shut up!" he looked up and listened, his eyes fearful. To Halley's surprise and relief, a volley of barking erupted and it was coming closer and closer.

"Damn!" Elmer said, dropping his hold and tearing out toward the ravine.

Halley ran in the opposite direction but had only gone a few feet when Blackie appeared. Halley squatted. "Git 'im!" she said, pointing in the direction Elmer had run. "Git 'im!"

Even as she spoke, she heard the crashing through the underbrush. Blackie heard it too and took off in that direction. Immediately, Halley was on her feet again. Then she was on the trail and running toward Belton. She was crying with both fear and relief and could not seem to stop.

Then the sound and the smell of the mill were in the air. Minutes later she was in town, and she could see Shropshire's Store across the street and down a piece. Halley stopped in front of the Methodist Church and sat on a low stone wall along the sidewalk. She had to compose herself before going to the store. If she told what had happened, it would be all over town before the day was out. By tomorrow, the story would be that Elmer actually did rape her. No matter what she said, from then on, that story would follow her. If she lived to be ninety, the main thing the people around Belton would have to say about her was, "That there's the woman that got raped by that Logan man."

Well, they would never be able to say that about her because nobody was ever going to know anything happened.

15. A Surprise

"HELLO," SOMEONE CALLED.

Halley looked up to see Richard Bonner. He pulled his car alongside the sidewalk and stopped. Folded spreads and spools of yarn were piled high in the back seat.

"You have your own route now," she said.

Nodding, Richard got out, and sat down beside her. "Can I add you to my list of tufters?"

Halley shook her head. "My grandmother's still sick."

Richard put an arm around her and pulled her closer. He smelled wonderful—clean and nice—but she was nervous from Elmer's attack. She pulled away.

He smiled. "Anything I can help with?"

"Nothing," Halley said. She folded her arms. She could hardly think. His right hand touched her shoulder. How different from Elmer's rough touch. I'm safe, she told herself.

He's not like Elmer.

"You sure you're okay?"

"Yeah," she said.

At that moment Halley spotted a familiar truck with a house on back. "The picture woman is still here," she said, glad to change the subject. "I figured she'd left months ago. What on earth is keeping her around so long?"

"I think she wants to show the rest of the country what it's like to live here in the mountains," Richard said.

"You mean show what hicks we are."

"No, I don't think it's like that for Theodora. I think she studies people the way some people read books or raise crops."

Richard's hand was on her shoulder again, and Halley was astonished at her own reaction. She wanted him to kiss her. Her entire body was a fever of wanting. In that moment she understood why girls "got in trouble"—why Bootsie let things go so far with Stan. Frightened, she pulled away, and this time she stood. She wasn't ready for this.

"Right now I've got to go ask Tate Shropshire to buy my mother's wedding band." She stopped, wishing she had thought before speaking.

"You're selling your mother's wedding ring?"

Halley pulled out the ring and the drawing of Robbie's foot. "Mama wants me to get rubber boots, candy, and a toy for my brother's Christmas, and we don't have any money. I'm afraid Tate Shropshire will never pay enough for all that. But I've got to ask."

"I think he'd do it for me," Richard said thoughtfully. "Why don't you let me handle it while you wait outside."

"I couldn't ask you to do that," Halley answered, looking at the hand that had been on her shoulder. The nails were clean and trimmed. The fingers were muscular and strong.

"You didn't ask. I'm offering. Come on."

He opened the door with a bow and Halley got in. She felt about as graceful as Sukie pulling her foot out of the mud.

Halley rode with Richard to the store and waited on the bench out front. He was back in only a few minutes, handing her two boxes and a bag. "Here you are, the boots, a top, and some candy," he said, "and here's your change."

"Ten dollars!" said Halley. "I can't believe he gave you this much!"

"I'm a regular customer," he replied. He did another bow. "Anything else I can do for you?"

"No," she said, still looking at the money. "I've got to go in and buy some things for my grandparents."

"And I've got to head out on my route," Richard said. He took her hand and squeezed it. "Don't mention to Shropshire that the ring I sold was yours."

"I won't," Halley said.

"And it'd probably be best to leave the shoes and things on the bench while you go in."

Richard squeezed her hand once more and got in his car. With a wave he was gone. Halley watched him drive away.

If only she thought like Dimple, this might be her way of escaping the Franklins. Being married to Richard wouldn't be bad, she thought. He probably made a good living. He had a car. He was good-looking.

"That *can't* be your boyfriend," someone said. Halley turned to see one of the town girls she'd seen on her first day in Belton. The girl looked at Halley up and down, from her faded head scarf down to her muddy shoes.

"And why not?" Halley asked, looking right back at the girl. She even managed to wrinkle her nose the same way the girl did.

With a toss of her head the girl walked away and Halley went inside the store. It smelled a lot like the rolling store where she traded in Alpha Springs. And it was almost as crowded with merchandise. The dimness was lit by a number of light bulbs hanging on cords from the high ceilings. A couple of men warmed themselves by the big pot bellied stove in the center of the store, and three women were doing their shopping. A young man in an apron was stacking canned goods on a shelf.

Tate Shropshire leaned over the counter next to the cash register. "How do, young lady. Can I help you?"

"I need five pounds of coffee," she said.

"Your face looks familiar," said Shropshire. "I can near about say your name."

"I'm Halley Owenby," she told him.

"Oh yeah. Your father was Jim Owenby. Sorry for your loss."

"Thanks," Halley said stiffly. "How much will I owe you?"

The noon whistle sounded as Halley started out. The mill workers began streaming out of the building, headed for the gate. The ones who lived in the mill village would rush home to eat. Some would go to the store to buy moon pies or candy bars and soft drinks. The rest, like her mother, would try to find a spot of sunshine outside and eat something from home. If Halley hurried, she might speak to Kate. She needed to tell enough about Elmer, so her mother would know to watch out for him. Even though he was likely to be too afraid of the dog to try anything on Kate, she had to make sure.

Halley picked up the bag with the boots, top, and candy, and headed for the gate. A truck passed her and parked just short of the gate, so Halley would not be able to see her mother until she got past the truck.

"Hey, Halley!" called Bootsie, who was in the crowd headed

home for lunch. She waved her sister and mother on and stopped to give Halley a quick hug. "Everything okay, honey?"

Halley nodded and held up her packages. "Just getting Christmas for Robbie."

"Good!"

It was the first time she had seen Bootsie since the day Stan ran them off the road. She stole a look at Bootsie's waist and whispered, "Did you for sure lose the baby?"

Bootsie nodded sorrowfully. "For sure, not that I had any doubt. I was with my mama when she lost one. I'm telling myself that I'll have more babies. Gid's babies."

Halley squeezed her hand. "I'm glad we're going to have you in the family."

"Same here," said Bootsie. "But I gotta hurry or I won't have time to eat."

Halley turned back toward the mill gate. The truck was still there, but the motor was running. At that moment the passenger side door slammed, and the truck pulled on down the street a short distance. It stopped and the motor turned off.

Halley looked at the people in the yard around the mill. They were collected in groups of twos and threes, eating lunch. Her mother was not among them. She looked again. Surely her mother had not stayed inside with all the lint. She'd promised Halley to always eat outside if weather permitted. That at least gave her thirty minutes of fresh air.

Halley went right up to the gate guard. "I'm looking for my mother, Kate Owenby," she said.

Without turning, the guard pointed down the street to the truck.

Puzzled, Halley really looked at the truck for the first time and realized it was familiar. It was Bud Gravitt's truck. Then she realized that the person who'd just gotten in on the passenger side was Kate. Even from where she stood, Halley could see her mother's face. Kate was smiling. But it didn't make *her* feel like smiling. In fact, she was angry. Her mother didn't have time to buy Robbie's gift, but she had time to carry on with Bud Gravitt in his truck. She probably thought Halley would be through shopping and gone before noon.

All the angry, hurtful things she wanted to say boiled up inside her. That Kate had betrayed her father's memory. That she was shaming them all by sneaking around with a man this soon after both their spouses had died.

Finally, she turned away and headed for the trail back to the Franklin place. Her feet felt like lead. She did not even think of Elmer until she reached the place where she had last seen him. There was no sign of the boy or the dog, and all traces of the smoke had vanished.

‖‖‖

16. Bud Gravitt Returns

HALLEY SPENT PART OF FRIDAY WRITING AND REWRITING HER letter to Martha Berry in Rome, Georgia.

She wrote it three times before she was satisfied. She made sure to mention that Gid Franklin was her uncle. She told how she'd longed for an education beyond the eight years she had.

The letter was finally as good as she could make it. All she had in the way of an address for Miss Berry was the city and state. Maybe the post office in Rome would know Miss

Berry and her school.

Halley debated with herself about a return address. Without an explanation, she could not ask Miss Berry to send a reply to Clarice Calvin. She finally decided she had to use her real address and take a chance that she or Robbie could get to the mail every day ahead of Pa Franklin.

Before she lost her courage, Halley planned to take the letter to the mailbox along with pennies for postage. Then she had another thought. What if the mailman had not come when Pa Franklin returned from visiting sick folks? He was sure to stop at the mailbox. Best to wait. She put the letter in her pocket.

Sure enough, Pa Franklin was back well before dinnertime.

"How was ever'body?" asked Ma Franklin as her husband backed up to the stove.

"Tolerable. But I hear tell that oldest Logan boy is laid up."

"Elmer? What's wrong?"

Halley's heart leaped up even before he answered. She hadn't spared the boy a thought since it happened. She had told the dog to get him, but she figured Elmer would climb a tree or fight the dog off. And too, thoughts of her mother and Bud Gravitt had crowded out most other worries.

"Elmer's bad off," Pa Franklin said. "Got chewed up something fierce by a pack of dogs, he says."

"A *bunch* of dogs?" said Halley.

"That's what the boy said. Didn't know any of the dogs, he says. Says he run up on 'em in the woods behind their house, and they all jumped 'im. Nobody else seen any strange dogs around. Sounds fishy to me."

"And he's bad off, you say?" asked Ma Franklin.

Pa Franklin nodded. "Doc Graham had to sew up an arm and a leg and a big place on his face."

Halley gasped. Elmer had done wrong, but she hadn't wanted to cripple him. It was easy to understand why he didn't tell the truth. Then he could be in real trouble for trespassing and building a fire on someone else's property. Of course, if Pa Franklin found out what Elmer had been burning, the boy would be in even more trouble.

On Saturday Bootsie came home from the mill with Kate. She was like sunshine in the gloomy house. "Kate's gonna help me make my wedding dress," she announced after saying her hellos and giving Robbie the ball she had brought for him.

Halley promptly took the ball. "Not until you go outside," she whispered.

"It ain't going to be no real fancy wedding," Bootsie went on, "but I wanted a new dress, and I know Kate can make dresses prettier than Sears and Roebuck on that sewing machine of hers." Much to Pa Franklin's disappointment, Kate had moved the machine to the kitchen the day before.

"Don't brag until you see what I turn out," Kate said, but Halley could see she was pleased. She had once loved sewing. Pa Franklin grunted from the table where he was waiting for Halley to set out dinner. "The Bible says take no thought of what ye shall wear."

Halley almost laughed, thinking about *his* clothing.

"Well, the Bible's right, like always," Bootsie said. "And I ain't taking *worried* thought. I'll bet God is just tickled pink ever'time he sees us human beings taking happy thought about something good. And there ain't nothing but good in me and Gid getting married. He loves me and I love him." She laid her fabric on Kate's sewing machine and pulled off her coat.

"You sure are handy with deciding what God likes and don't like," Pa Franklin said.

Bootsie laughed and began setting out plates as if she were at home. "Not near as handy as you, Mr. Franklin! Sounds as if you and me was heaven meant to be kinfolks."

Without waiting for a reply, she turned to Halley. "Wish I could ask you to stand up for me, but my cousin's going to drive us to Calhoun for the wedding. Me and Gid figured we'd have a better chance of keeping it secret that way. We'll stay a couple nights and then come here."

"We'd be glad to have you," Ma Franklin said before her husband could say anything about more mouths to feed.

"When Gid goes back to the CCC, I'll go back to my sister's."

That part of the plan, at least, got a big nod of approval from Pa Franklin.

Halley put the beans, potatoes, and cornbread on the table, and they sat down to eat. While Pa Franklin yawned, Bootsie and Kate discussed exactly how they would make the dress, picking up the Sears and Roebuck catalog every now and then to look for details on sleeves, collars, and length. Pa Franklin was snoring in his rocker by the time the table was cleared for laying out fabric.

Kate and Bootsie had even more fun cutting the dress pieces. Halley was a little envious of the enjoyment the two of them had together. It was as if Kate were the same age as Bootsie, and Halley was older than either of them.

"Take some of my canned soup to the Logans," said Ma Franklin, when Halley was ready to go clean the church.

Halley wanted to refuse but knew she could not. All the way to the Logan house she thought of things she might have done differently when Elmer had her pinned against the tree. But there was no plan that would have both saved herself and prevented his injuries.

The Logan house was just like the family—unkempt. The back porch had completely fallen in. Enough of the ruins had been cleared away for a path to the back door, and the rest lay where it had fallen. The front porch was headed for the same fate, and one side was already sagging too much to use.

One of the smaller children discovered her arrival. "Company!" the child yelled and threw open the door.

Lillie Mae Logan met her. Far advanced in pregnancy now, she had on the same dress Halley had last seen her in. It was very short in front because the waist rode above her belly. The hem had not been repaired.

Halley handed her the two jars of soup. "From Ma Franklin," she said. "How's Elmer?"

Lillie Mae looked at the soup eagerly. "Hurting pretty bad."

Halley looked toward the bed where Elmer lay but hardly recognized him. His face was swollen and bandaged, and so were both arms and legs. The bandages were bloody. The main thing she noticed, however, were his eyes. They were bright with rage. "Git out!" he said.

"I'm sorry you're hurt," she told him. "But it's not my fault." She went very near his bed and spoke in a low voice. "I hate it about the dog, Elmer. But I have to tell you, dogs have always favored me and my family. They look out for us, even when they're not our dogs. They'll hunt people down who mistreat us."

Halley turned to Lillie Mae. "You might want to ask Carrie Gowder and her granddaughter, Opal, for help. They sure helped my grandmother."

"Git out!" said Elmer, and Halley left.

SUNDAY CAME, AND WITH it Bud Gravitt. He arrived early when Kate was pulling apple pies from the oven. She obviously had been expecting him, for she had made egg custard too, ignoring her father's complaints about the waste of good eggs and milk. She set both pies and custard in the warming oven.

"I figured I'd get here early and drive you all to church," Bud said.

"Thank you just the same, but one of my deacons allus picks me up when the weather's bad," said Pa Franklin.

"Robbie and me will ride with you," Kate said. "Ma's not strong enough to get out in the cold yet, and Halley will need to stay here and cook the rest of dinner."

"I hate for Halley to miss church," Ma Franklin said from her rocker.

"It's okay," Halley replied, and it was. Except for missing the Calvin girls, Halley was glad to stay home. She was also glad not to be a witness to her mother and Bud Gravitt out in public as a couple.

"I don't know what I'd do without this girl," said Ma Franklin. "She cooks and washes and irons, and she don't ever have a day off."

Kate looked from her mother to Halley as if only now realizing the truth of the words.

Soon those going to church left, and the house was quiet. Pa Franklin must have really gotten fired up with his preaching. It was a good bit past noon when the trucks pulled up outside.

A few minutes later they sat down to the finest dinner Halley had ever seen on the Franklin table. Kate had killed two chickens that morning for Halley to fry. Bud Gravitt was suitably impressed. He took pains to compliment each thing he suspected Kate had prepared. For once Pa Franklin paid no attention to Robbie or his manners. Instead, he went to great lengths to point out Kate's faults.

"Kate's not much of a farm hand," he said right after the

blessing. "Never was, as far as that goes, but Jim finished ruining her. He was bad to let her set up in the house when hoeing or picking was to be done."

"Jim had the right idea," said Bud Gravitt. "Lots of farm women break their health working crops and trying to run a house all at the same time. I'm not saying a woman shouldn't help out in a tight, but as an ever'day thing, she's got enough work keeping the house going."

Later Pa Franklin said, "Seems to me a woman can go too far in school for her own good. Just to show you what I'm talking about, Kate here can add up a column of figures long as my arm, *in her head*. Always thinking she knows ever'thing."

Bud shrugged. "Man or woman, I never did see no advantage to ignorance."

Just before apple pie and custard were served, Pa Franklin said, "Kate's as tight as a gourd when it comes to money."

This was comical, Halley thought, coming from Pa Franklin. Who could be tighter than him? And these days when did Kate ever have any money to be tight with? All she had was the ten dollars Halley had given her from the sale of her ring. So far she had not given that to Pa Franklin, but that was probably only because he didn't know she had it.

"A penny saved is a penny earned," Bud Gravitt said.

"But she can throw away sometimes too," Pa Franklin went on, "just like when she was giving away groceries to the Logans."

"There's a time to save and a time to give," Gravitt said.

Pa Franklin looked at Bud Gravitt sharply before turning his full attention to his pie.

As soon as Bud left, Pa Franklin began to criticize *him*.

"His ears are so big, I expected him to commence braying just any minute. Come to think on it, he has teeth like a mule, too. Course I reckon that don't stop him from talking pretty."

Kate did not respond, so Pa Franklin began to needle Halley.

"How you like your new stepdaddy, girl? You think you had it hard around here, wait until you're cooking, washing, and cleaning for the whole Gravitt mob. You'll be wishing and praying you was back here."

Little as she liked the idea of her mother and Bud Gravitt as a match, Halley could not bring herself to side with her grandfather.

"Are you going to marry Mr. Gravitt?" asked Robbie.

"Not as far as I know," said Kate.

Halley could not help noticing a smug look on her mother's face that gave the lie to her words. Two letters arrived from Bud Gravitt that week. Halley received no mail at all.

17. Christmas

NONE OF THE MARRIED FRANKLIN CHILDREN CAME FOR CHRISTmas. Among them all only Ralph sometimes had the use of a motor vehicle, and his boss's truck cab wasn't big enough to hold all Ralph's family. Only during warm weather could passengers ride in back.

Gid arrived on Christmas Eve, but he hardly looked like his old self. He had become good-looking. He'd gained weight and put on muscle. He even looked taller. He was full of stories about life in camp and all he was learning in his classes. Pa

Franklin grunted and snorted about waste of time and the devil's work, but everyone else was interested.

Ma Franklin finally dared bring up the question Halley had been wanting to ask: "Is it as good as if you'd gone to Miss Berry's school?"

Gid studied a moment and then nodded. "Sometimes you just have to wait till it's the right time for a thing to happen."

Halley knew he was thinking about more than school. He was thinking of Bootsie, too.

After a short while Gid kissed his mother and announced he had to go see his girl. "Got to make wedding plans," he said. "Can we make room for Bootsie here tonight? Maybe her and Halley can share a pallet."

"You know she's welcome," said Ma Franklin.

CHRISTMAS MORNING CAME, AND Robbie was beside himself with joy over his gifts. In addition, Bootsie had bought him a jigsaw puzzle.

"*Your* present is coming a little later," Gid told Bootsie when they sat down to the breakfast table.

Bootsie squeezed his arm. "I already got all the present I want," she said.

"Well, I figure old mule ears ain't coming," Pa Franklin said to Kate when the meal was nearly over. "Probably too cheap to buy you a present. Or maybe he's off braying sweet nothings to some other widder woman closer to home."

Kate ignored him, but Pa Franklin's good cheer continued right on up until Garnetta arrived.

"I didn't know *she* was coming," said Pa Franklin.

"I invited her," said Gid.

Garnetta was alone this time. She brought food. There were two cakes—one coconut and one chocolate. There was candy, and there was fruit. The oranges smelled like Christmas to Halley.

"The fruit is from Bud Gravitt," Garnetta said, "a special gift for Kate."

Pa Franklin quickly put down the orange he had just picked up.

"Bud said he wished he could be here, but he's having Christmas with his young'uns at his sister's house." She slipped a small box into Gid's pocket.

Gid cleared his throat. "I got a little something I want to give my bride-to-be while ever'body's here to admire it." He pulled the box from his pocket, opened it and took out a ring. It had a ruby and what looked like diamonds on either side.

"Oh!" Bootsie said, clasping her hands. "For me!"

Gid nodded. "It was Garnetta's from her late husband, Barney, and she wanted us to have it."

"It's beautiful!" Bootsie said. "Put it on my finger, Gid." He did, and Bootsie kissed him, and then Garnetta.

Deacon Pruitt arrived to pick up Pa Franklin for church.

Garnetta let Gid drive her car, and she stayed to help Halley while the rest went to church. "I think Mama is going to marry Bud Gravitt," Halley whispered when Ma Franklin dozed off in the sudden quiet.

Garnetta continued cutting up chicken. "Your mother could do worse. Bud is a good man and a good provider."

Halley began peeling potatoes. "But Daddy's only been dead five months, and Bud's wife has been gone three."

"Do you think waiting will bring them back? Seems to me Kate and Bud need each other."

After a long silence Halley confided her hopes for going off to school.

"I've heard of that school. You go."

"I've not been invited yet. But, if I am, what about leaving Robbie? Pa Franklin is too hard on him."

"And everybody else," said Garnetta, setting her mouth in a deep frown. "Dimple told me about the money he took from you. I sometimes wonder if that man has any good left in him."

Halley nodded. She felt the same. "So who'll look out for Robbie, if I'm gone?"

"I think that's going to work itself out. Anyway, you need to let that boy handle some things for himself and take some knocks. How is he going to learn to be a man?"

Just like Clarice had said, thought Halley.

Ma Franklin roused up. "Who you talking about?" she asked.

"I'm talking about everybody," said Garnetta. "I was just telling Halley that the way we get strong enough to make it in this world is to learn to take hard knocks and go on."

"That's the Lord's truth," said Ma Franklin. "And I've had many a knock in my life." She looked hard at Garnetta. "But I didn't figure *you* had. Seem like to me you've had it pretty easy. And you look mighty handsome to boot."

"I've had my own hard knocks," Garnetta said. "And whatever looks I have, I'd trade in a minute to have some children and grandchildren like yours."

Ma Franklin's face softened. She wiped her eyes on her apron. "Yes, I've been blessed."

"Webb did a good day's work when he got you to marry him."

Ma Franklin shook her head. "I was nothing special then. Ain't now."

"Oh, yes, you are," said Garnetta. "You are giving and loving and kind. And you believe in Webb Franklin even more than he believes in himself. I don't think he could manage without you."

"Thank you," said Ma Franklin.

CHRISTMAS DINNER WAS READY when Pa Franklin and the rest returned from church. The meal was just as good as Halley had expected it to be. And when they had eaten and washed dishes, Garnetta declared that it was time for Robbie to play the piano. "I think we need some Christmas carols to finish off the day."

"That would finish it all right," Pa Franklin said, but nobody paid him any mind.

Robbie practically ran to the piano. "First, I'm playing 'Beulah Land' for Ma Franklin," he said. "I practiced one day when Pa Franklin was gone."

They all sang together except for Pa Franklin. It seemed to Halley that some knot deep inside her heart was loosening a little.

18. Everything Changes

HALLEY KNEW THE WEEK FOLLOWING CHRISTMAS WAS BOUND to be miserable. Bootsie and Gid planned to leave to get married on December twenty-sixth, and Kate was off from work without pay until the first Monday in the new year. Pa Franklin made no secret of his displeasure with both circumstances.

He was muttering and fuming Monday morning when Bootsie's cousin Royce Cox arrived in his car. Royce was taking the happy couple to Calhoun for the wedding. Bootsie and Gid shook Pa Franklin's hand and hugged the rest of the family before heading out to the car. Their bubbling over happiness only served to further rankle Pa Franklin. He went to the porch with the rest, though his glowering face was enough to dampen all joy.

"Git out of the way, Golly," he said, kicking at the dog. Golly was sniffing his way toward Robbie, the best source of petting and food.

"Fetch some stove wood, Robbie," Halley said, to head off trouble.

Pa Franklin grunted. "What little there is to fetch, you mean. Reckon the ones of us staying home where we orta be are near about down to splinters and logs too big to git in the stove."

Gid laughed. "Pa, I split some yesterday and I'll split more when I get back." He opened the car door for Bootsie and bowed. The suit Garnetta Miller had given him from her late husband's wardrobe was a little big, but Halley thought he looked grand anyway.

Bootsie giggled up at him and smoothed the skirt of her new dress. Then she turned her radiant smile on her future father-in-law. "Turn loose some of that CCC money and hire some help, Mr. Franklin."

Pa Franklin grunted with disgust. "I don't have no time to git out and hunt no labor. Not with ever'thing else I got on me."

At that moment Sukie, the cow, gave out a bellow from the barn. She'd been acting up since the night before. "Hear that fool cow?" Pa Franklin said. "She can't wait for a warm spell to come into heat. No-siree! She's got to be took over to Temp Little's house to be serviced today, when they's near about ice on the ground."

Halley caught the look Ma Franklin shot her husband. Things like breeding animals just weren't discussed in front of women and children. Especially not in the Franklin household.

Royce snorted with laughter. "From what I hear about that cow, preacher, you could just turn 'er loose. I s'pect the old gal would likely find 'er own way over to Temp's pasture."

Gid got into the car. He and Bootsie were both laughing behind their hands as they drove away.

"Why does Sukie want to go to Temp Little's house?" asked Robbie.

Ma Franklin's face was as red as Kate's. "Never mind," they both said together.

"Fetch the wood, like I told you," said Halley.

They were hardly back in the kitchen when Golly let out another volley of barking.

"Gid and Bootsie musta forgot something," said Ma Franklin, shuffling toward the front window.

Halley heard footsteps and ran to the door just in time to let Robbie in with a load of wood. "Mr. Gravitt's here," he said.

"*Again?*" said Pa Franklin.

Moments later Bud Gravitt was in the kitchen, shaking Pa Franklin's unwilling hand. "I've brung you a truck load of split wood as a Christmas present," he said, "and I'll bring you another load next time I come."

Ma Franklin thanked him profusely. "Ain't that just like an answer to a prayer, Old Man," she said to her husband.

"I reckon," Pa Franklin muttered. "Much obliged."

Bud smiled as if he'd received an enthusiastic thank-you. "I'm going to unload it for you before taking Kate over to my sister's house."

Pa Franklin stiffened. "Taking Kate where?"

"I'm going to see Bud's baby," Kate quickly explained, "Will."

"Can I go, too?" asked Robbie.

"Sounds like a good idee to me," Pa Franklin said, but Kate shook her head.

As soon as Kate and Bud Gravitt left, Pa Franklin began criticizing them both. "Looks like Kate's done lost ever bit of judgment she ever had. As for that long hungry she's a-going with, he don't have enough sense to know he ain't welcome here."

Ma Franklin ventured a meek defense. "Well, he brung wood."

"Not enough to pay for half the groceries he puts down. And in the meantime he's blackening Kate's reputation."

"I guess that's so," Ma Franklin admitted.

Halley felt her grandfather's eyes turn in her direction, willing her to say something, compelling her to line up on his side. It was the same almost hypnotic power he used when he asked sinners to come to the altar and repent.

Halley steeled herself to resist. She could not do what he wanted. She *would* not. Though she had no great affection for Bud Gravitt, she would not be her grandfather's ally. Not ever.

In silence, Halley put the sweet potatoes in the oven to bake for dinner and stirred the turnip greens and beans. Then she returned to the ironing she had begun right after breakfast. All without meeting her grandfather's gaze. All without saying a word.

Finally, he gave up and spoke. "You'd think Gravitt would consider Kate's reputation. Fur as that goes, you'd expect *Kate* to think of it. What kind of example is she setting—strollicking all over the country with a man just widdered, and her own husband barely cold in the ground! Her own husband that she *claimed* to love. The man her young'uns claimed *they* loved."

Halley felt the old man's gaze again, but Sukie saved her. From the barn came the cow's insistent bellow, and at last Pa Franklin stood.

"I can tell Temp Little one thing—I ain't paying him nothing until I see a living calf out of that heifer. And if Sukie proves good at calving, it'll be the first thing she's good at."

Ma Franklin put out a hand to her husband. "Now, Old Man, it ain't fair to expect 'im to keep the cow three days, and feed her, for nothing. And Temp might not be so willing next time you have a cow needing serviced."

Pa Franklin seemed as astonished as Halley at Ma Franklin's boldness. "Who's boss around here," he asked, "you or me?"

Pa Franklin left a few minutes later and peace descended on the household. While knitting socks Ma Franklin began talking about when she was young and going to long ago singings and corn shuckings. "Did I tell you about when me and Webb won first prize at a square dance?"

Robbie yawned and nodded.

"I went hunting with him, too, sometimes," she went on. "One time, I recollect, I held some of the dogs so your grandfather could go look for his lead dog. It was sort of scary being in them dark woods by myself except for the hounds . . ."

Robbie yawned again and headed outside. He slipped a biscuit out of the warming oven and grabbed the knotted keep-away rope from behind the wood box before opening the door, so Halley knew he was going to play with Golly.

While Halley worked her way to the bottom of the ironing pile, Ma Franklin talked on. It seemed to Halley that the young man in the stories was a different person from the one

Ma Franklin now claimed as a husband. The young Webb Franklin sounded like *fun*. Once he had even taken part in a horse race.

"He didn't make no bets, understand," said Ma Franklin, looking at Halley over her glasses, "though we did hear tell of other folks gambling on it. And the ones that gambled on my Webb won." She smiled shyly. "I reckon you might say I won my bet on him, too."

The arrival of Mr. Calvin and his daughter Lacey put an end to the stories.

"Lacey and me have come to invite Halley to a little Christmas social my girls are giving at our house today," Mr. Calvin said after an exchange of greetings.

Lacey winked at her, and Halley's heart lifted for a moment before sinking again. There was no chance in the world she would be allowed to go.

"Me too?" asked Robbie, who had followed the Calvins in. "Can I go?"

Nobody answered Robbie. Ma Franklin's eyes darted to the chair where her husband usually sat and then to Halley. "I don't know."

"Halley's been working mighty hard," said Mr. Calvin, "especially since you've been ailing."

Ma Franklin nodded. "That's so."

"Me and my wife'll be there the whole time, and I'll fetch Halley home by sundown."

Ma Franklin looked toward the door, shaking her head. "I wish the Old Man was here to say."

"Please let her come," said Lacey. "We're going to sing and play games and make candy. We're going to play the victrola Daddy got us for Christmas. We may even do some square dancing."

Square dancing? Halley wondered if that meant boys would be there too? She dared not ask.

"Pa and Ma Franklin used to square dance when they was young," said Robbie.

Ma Franklin smiled. "I hadn't thought of it like that. I reckon it wouldn't hurt."

"Can I go too?" Robbie asked again.

Ma Franklin shook her head. "I'll need you to fetch wood and water."

"And I need you to check the mailbox," Halley reminded him. Robbie was under strict instructions to put any mail in his pocket until Halley could go through it looking for her answer from Martha Berry.

"You can come over tomorrow," Mr. Calvin promised Robbie, "or the next day."

Halley practically danced her way to the far room to change clothes and comb her hair. If only she had known earlier, she could have tried to curl her hair a bit. She pinched her cheeks and bit her lips for color. Minutes later she was in the truck.

Music and singing were pouring out of the Calvin house when they arrived, and when the truck pulled to a stop, young people swarmed out of the house to the porch. Richard was among them. It seemed his smile was for her alone.

"It's Halley!" Clarice said.

Then they were all in the Calvin parlor and Halley was singing with them. It had been a long time since her heart felt so light and happy.

The happiness continued through dinner. When they were finishing their apple pie, Clarice said, "Richard learned ballroom dancing in Atlanta."

A murmur ran around the table. "Atlanta!" "Ballroom dancing!"

"And as big a flirt as you are, I know you charmed ever' woman in the ballroom," Eva said.

Everyone laughed while Richard shrugged and put on a "who me?" face.

"Richard promised to teach *us* ballroom dancing," said Lacey.

Richard smiled modestly. "I'll show what little I know."

Back in the parlor a short while later, Clarice's boyfriend, Homer, wound up the victrola while Clarice chose a record from the collection stored in the bottom of the cabinet.

"The main thing is to listen to the music and let it tell you when and how to move your feet," Richard said as everyone circled around.

"It won't tell *me* anything," said Halley.

"Yes, it will." Richard reached for Halley's hand. "Let me show you."

At his touch Halley felt the same warmth and wanting she had felt the week before—and the same fear. She also felt clumsy and awkward. She didn't want to embarrass herself in front of everyone. She pulled away, folding her arms. "I can't dance."

Clarice nudged her forward. "Come on, Halley. Don't take it so serious. None of us know, either."

Unwillingly, Halley allowed Richard to take her hand and pull her to the center of the room, facing him. His right hand encircled her waist and his left hand took her right. "Put your left hand on my shoulder," he instructed.

Halley became very aware of the smell of shaving soap and hair tonic and starch. She was aware too of how damp and sweaty her hands had become, and how hot her cheeks were.

The music started. "Step-step, slide." Richard said, maneuvering Halley to move with him. "Step-step, slide."

Halley lurched and stepped on his foot. "Sorry," she said as she stepped on his foot again. She felt as stiff as a two-by-four.

Richard smiled encouragingly. "Step-step, slide."

"Sorry," Halley said again, her face burning. "Sorry."

"Stop apologizing," he whispered. "Step-step, slide."

"I'm going to sit down," Halley whispered, trying to tug her hand free.

"No, you're not," Richard answered, tightening his grip. "Step-step, slide. Step-step, slide. You're getting better."

Sure enough, she'd moved several times without stomping on his feet. Some tension inside her began to loosen. Then Clarice and Homer began dancing beside them, and Halley relaxed more, and then a little more. Suddenly it did seem as if her feet *were* learning from the music where to go. She and Richard were moving mostly together around and around the room. Step-step, slide. Maybe someday they would dance together in Atlanta and she would wear a long gown then. Richard would wear a tuxedo, of course. Step-step, slide.

Time passed, and the record changed, but Richard asked no one else to dance. She could feel the other girls in the room looking at her with envy. She heard, without really hearing, the Calvin dogs barking out in the yard, the front door opening, heavy footsteps coming down the hallway.

Then a loud voice demanded, "What is going on here?"

Halley swung around to see her grandfather standing in the doorway. His face was furious. Halley backed away from Richard. If only she could disappear.

The older Calvins came running from the kitchen. "The young folks are just dancing," said Mr. Calvin.

"I *seen* what they're doing with my own eyes," said Pa Franklin. "The devil's work! I don't know about your girls, but my granddaughter ain't going to take no part in such doings."

He stopped and looked hard at Richard. "Who *are* you?"

Mrs. Calvin stepped forward and put one hand on Richard's shoulder. "This is Richard Bonner—a fine young man. He and his father hire people to tuft bedspreads."

"And you're letting him carry on with my granddaughter!"

Mr. Calvin's face turned to stone. "I don't call this carrying on."

"We were *dancing*," Halley said.

Richard stepped forward. "Sir, you don't have a thing to worry about. Halley and I are just friends. I have a sweetheart already, and I'm not looking for another one."

Halley felt her face blaze. She'd made a bigger idiot of herself than her grandfather had. She shoved her way by Richard, her grandfather, and Mr. and Mrs. Calvin. Grabbing her coat from the bench in the hallway, she rushed out the front door into air so cold it stung her cheeks. She didn't care. She wanted to be cold.

Her grandfather caught her at the edge of the yard. "Hold up, young lady," he bellowed. "You're not getting out of my sight. You done proved you can't be trusted."

Walking as fast as she could, Halley let him rant until he was so out of breath he could not talk. When they passed the church, Halley saw Theodora Langford's truck parked off to one side. Theodora had her camera set to photograph the cemetery with its leaning stones and wooden crosses.

"Reckon you aim to turn out like her," Pa Franklin said, jerking his head toward the photographer.

"I could do worse," Halley answered, "and it would be a pure relief to quit worrying about what people say."

Her grandfather made no reply, but by the time they reached the cut off to the Franklin place, he had started preaching again. "You can forget about going to the store anymore," he said, stopping at the mailbox. He reached in and came out empty handed. Halley rejoiced in his disappointment that the CCC check still hadn't come.

"You can't be trusted to go to Belton," he went on.

"Fine with me," Halley said.

"You're not going to the Calvins no more either."

"Fine." Halley didn't want to see the Calvins any more— not after they'd seen her humiliated by both her grandfather and Richard.

When they reached the edge of the Franklin yard, Halley saw her grandmother waiting at the kitchen window. The old lady's eyes were red and her entire body downcast. For a moment Halley forgot her own anger and embarrassment.

"Don't fuss on Grandma anymore," she begged. "I'll take all the blame."

"Ain't you free-hearted?" her grandfather said sarcastically. "You'll take whatever blame I say. You ain't the boss around here." He swung around toward the pasture where Halley suddenly realized Robbie and Golly were running. Robbie had the keep-away rope in his hand, holding it out behind him. The two behaved as though racing the wind, their feet barely touching the ground. Then Golly wheeled about and spotted his master. He halted at once and his tail drooped. Suddenly he was an old dog again.

"How many times do I have to tell that boy to leave Golly be?" Pa Franklin said. "He's turning my guard dog into a lap pet." Cupping his hands to his mouth, he bellowed, "You, boy! Git to the house."

On entering the kitchen Halley saw her mother had returned. Kate was starting supper. With a fresh audience, Pa Franklin found a new burst of indignation. "Your daughter went out strollicking. Good thing I went after her," he said.

"This girl here was hugged up to that boy that puts out the bedspread work."

"Mr. Bonner's son," Halley explained. "We were only dancing."

Kate said nothing and neither did Ma Franklin.

"Dancing?" Pa Franklin mocked. "Oh, is *that* what they call it now?"

"*You* danced when you were young," Halley said, "and you raced horses and . . ." She broke off at the sight of her grandmother's face. She'd gotten her grandmother into deeper trouble. Pa Franklin turned on his wife.

"You been running your mouth," he said. At that moment Robbie burst into the kitchen and went straight to Halley. Digging into his pocket, he brought out two letters and handed them to her.

Before Halley could look at what she held, Pa Franklin snatched them from her hand.

"'Bout time that CCC check come," he said, slapping that letter on the table. "What!" he said. "Why's that Berry woman writing?"

"That's *my* mail," Halley protested as her grandfather ripped it open. "Mama, tell him he has no right."

Kate said nothing.

Her grandfather pulled out a folded sheet of paper and let the envelope flutter to the floor. Halley snatched it up. The return address said Berry Schools! Martha Berry had answered her. Was the answer "yes" or "no"? In her eagerness to know, she forgot her mother and grandmother. She tried to look at the letter as her grandfather read, but he pushed her away.

"Are they going to accept me?" she begged.

Pa Franklin wadded the letter and tossed it into the wood box. "Oh, she wants to accept you all right."

Halley was joyful. "She does? She really does?"

"That old maid can *accept you* all she wants and it won't make no difference. You're staying right here just like Gid when she wanted to take *him*. You ain't going nowhere but to the well or the barn. I've been entirely too easy on all of you. Well, I'm through being easy. For one thing, that piano is going out of this room." He looked around as though for some other privilege to take away. His eyes fell on the water bucket. "We need some water."

Turning, Halley grabbed her letter out of the wood box and then she got the water bucket. Robbie was right behind her as she headed through the dogtrot.

"I'm sorry," he said. "I didn't know he would take your letter."

"Then you're stupid," Halley said, setting the water bucket on the well housing and then heading for the main road.

"Please don't go away," said Robbie, still right behind her.

Halley turned on him. "Don't follow me," she yelled.

"Where are you going?" he asked.

"I don't know," she said. And she didn't. She only knew she had to get away from this place.

19. A Time to Choose

By the time Halley got to the county road she remembered Theodora. If only the woman was still at the church. She broke into a run. The wintry sunshine was sending long shadows across the road. A cold wind was picking up, making her clutch her coat against her chest. The coat stretched taut across her shoulders, and the frayed sleeves were too short. She blushed when she remembered that Richard had seen this coat. And she had actually thought he was *interested* in her.

"Idiot!" she said to herself. The Calvin girls had always said he was a big flirt, and that meant he tried to charm all the girls. She was nothing special. Why had she allowed herself to think she was? Because, she suddenly realized, she needed to be special to *somebody*. Nobody except her father had ever singled her out and made her feel above the crowd. All it took was a little attention from Richard, and she lost all the common sense she'd always taken pride in.

The church came into sight and Theodora was still there, but not for long. She was taking her camera off its tripod.

"Didn't I see you pass a little while ago?" Theodora asked when Halley drew near.

Halley nodded. "With my grandfather. I guess you could hear him pitching a fit at me."

"He's a minister, right?" said Theodora, opening the door to the house on the back of her truck.

"Yes," Halley answered, "and he's against dancing and about anything else that's fun or that he's too old to enjoy."

Theodora slid her camera into the little house. "So you

live with your grandparents?"

Halley nodded. "Mama thought she had to after Daddy died."

Theodora motioned her inside. "Come in out of the wind."

Halley entered. The room had a narrow bed, a tiny table, and one chair. Shelves in back were stacked with clothing, books, cooking utensils, camera supplies, and food stuff. Boxes of goods were stored under the bed and hung from the low ceiling in bags. Two small windows provided a bit of light. The place smelled of stale cigarette smoke. Except for that and being very cold, however, it seemed the kind of place Halley would like to retreat to when things grew unbearable in the Franklin household.

"Have a seat," said Theodora, indicating the only chair in the room.

A sudden gust of wind shook the truck and crept in around the door. Halley shivered. "How do you stay in here without heat? And how do you cook?"

"When cold weather started, I rented a room at a boarding house in Belton. As for cooking, I don't do any more of that than I can help even when the weather's good, and when I do cook, I do it outside, over a campfire."

Halley looked at the stack of photographs on the table. She recognized the top one at once. "The rolling store in Alpha Springs," she said. "There's Billy Shropshire weighing a chicken and Mollie Freeman frowning at the whole world."

"Look at all of them, if you wish," Theodora said. "I'll get you some light." She took a kerosene lamp out of a box beneath the bed. From another she took out a globe. Moments later the lamp was lit.

Halley looked at the pictures one by one, pausing long at the people and places she recognized. She studied the rolling store pictures and found Dimple in the background of one.

She came to the revival photos made at the Alpha Springs Methodist Church. There were pictures of Tate Shropshire's store in Belton. One showed mill workers eating lunch out in front of the store. Another photo showed high school students leaving the big two-story brick building where Halley had planned to study.

She came to a photo of Bootsie smoking a cigarette and smiling up at Stan. Halley thought she could detect the desperate effort the girl was making to win and hold him. You could almost see Bootsie's vision of what her life would be with this young man. And it was all a lie. Like me when I was dancing with Richard, she thought, and felt her face grow hot.

"Beautiful girl," said Theodora, leaning over Halley's shoulder to gaze at Bootsie.

Halley nodded. "She's married—I mean, going to marry—my Uncle Gid."

There were pictures of Belton Mill with its high brick walls and the tall fence surrounding it. "Looks like a jail," Halley murmured.

"Exactly what I was trying to convey," answered Theodora. "You are perceptive."

Halley wanted to ask what "perceptive" meant but didn't want to expose her ignorance. She continued studying the photos. One showed workers streaming in through the gate early in the morning. Another showed them streaming out at the end of the work day, covered with lint. Halley found her mother in the crowd. It must have been right after Kate hired on. Haggard and worried-looking, she had her hair pulled so tightly into its bun that her ears seemed to stand out. For the first time Halley realized that her mother no longer looked that way—not since Bud Gravitt had been calling on her. Now her hair swept halfway over her ears before being pulled back into a loose bun.

Halley forced herself to go to the next photo—a close-up of the gatekeeper. The man's face was angry and his mouth open. He pointed an accusing finger at the camera. In the next the hand was a fist.

"Some people don't want to see things the way they are," Theodora murmured. "They don't want *you* to see them either. You know, there are things people just don't see, until a photographer shows them."

It was true, Halley reluctantly admitted. Just like she had failed to see how much her mother had changed in such a short time. The next photo was apparently another lunch crowd. Even though the trees outside the mill were bare, some people stood about eating.

"I guess they're willing to take being cold for a few minutes of fresh air and freedom," Theodora said.

Halley studied the photo, looking without success for her mother or Bootsie. Then a truck just outside the gate caught her eye. It was Bud Gravitt's truck, and Bud Gravitt was in it. There was a woman sitting beside him. A pretty, laughing woman who looked so young and happy that for a moment Halley could not believe it was her mother.

Halley felt betrayed and angry all over again. She was angry that her mother could be that happy in the company of a man other than her father. But the anger went further, she suddenly realized. How could her mother be that joyful when Halley herself was miserable?

"I'm so glad for your mother," said Theodora.

"I'm not," Halley said. She flipped back through the photographs until they all became one picture of the Georgia mountain people—her people. Seeing the people in Alpha

Springs and the people in Belton, seeing farm people and mill people, seeing the ragged schoolchildren and the church congregations through this stranger's eyes, made Halley see everything differently, made her realize more fully than ever how hungry and poor they all were.

"Why do you do this?" she couldn't help asking. "Taking pictures like this, I mean? Do you make a lot of money?"

Theodora laughed. "Not so far. But I have hopes." She grew serious. "This is art, Halley, and artists don't generally make much money. They have to love what they're doing. I'm documenting a time and place. You might say I'm doing a history in pictures. Someday a hundred years from now people can look at these and know about these people. That's better than money."

"How do your folks take it, you living by yourself in this rolling house and traveling all over?" Halley blurted.

Theodora laughed. "Not too well, actually. Even up where I'm from people expect a woman to do housework, get married, and have babies—you know, stay in her place."

Halley nodded. "So how do you get away from all that and do what *you* want to do?"

Theodora pondered the question. Then she said, "You just refuse to live the life other people lay out for you. But there's a price to pay when you don't go by the rules. Nothing's fair and nothing's free. Make up your mind to that."

Halley laughed. "Oh, I know that already," she said, reaching into her pocket. "Here's what I want. It's my chance for a different life." She handed her crumpled Berry letter to Theodora. While the woman leaned close to the lamp and read, Halley rubbed her cold hands together. Her fingers were rough and cracked and her fingernails ragged.

"This is wonderful!" said Theodora. "Of course you are

going to this school."

Halley shook her head and swallowed hard. "They won't let me. My mother, my grandparents. And I'm not old enough to say what I want."

Theodora put her hand on Halley's arm. "But you *will* be. If you can just hang on, there'll come a time when you can choose and they can't stop you."

"How long do you plan to be around here?" Halley asked.

"Maybe until summer," said Theodora. "I've got a few more photographs to make. I want pictures of a wedding, a funeral, a newborn baby. And maybe spring planting."

"Wish I could go with you when you leave," Halley said.

"You know, I think you'd be good company. But you're a minor. They'd put me under the jail if I tried to take you."

"I know. I was only thinking out loud," Halley said quickly. She stood so abruptly that she rocked the table. The lamp teetered, and yellow circles of lamplight danced across the walls and ceiling.

Theodora stood and put a hand on Halley's arm. "Let your mother marry again," she said. "This is what she wants to choose. Don't take her choice away. Besides, her marrying again could free you."

Halley folded her letter and put it back in her pocket. "I've got to go." She went out into the twilight and did not look back. She heard the truck crank up a few minutes later, and as she turned by the Franklin mailbox, it passed by her. The horn tooted and Halley raised a hand without turning.

The wind was whipping the apple trees in the orchard. Then she saw a figure standing at the edge of the yard. It was Robbie and Golly was beside him. Suddenly he started running to meet her.

"I'm sorry," he said, throwing his arms around her. "About

your letter, I mean. I didn't think . . ."

Halley patted him. "I know. But you have to start thinking. I won't always be here to do your thinking for you."

"Pa Franklin rolled my piano into his room."

Halley shrugged. "Well, he wouldn't let you play it anyway."

"I drew the water," he said. "I told them I brought it in for you, that you went to the far room. Only Mama went back there and found out the truth. She didn't say nothing, but I think she's mad."

Well, I can bear it, Halley thought. Theodora was right—there *would* come a time when she could choose and would not have to obey anybody. Her real life—the one she would choose herself—was waiting for her.

|||||||||||||||||||||||||||||||||||||||||||||||||||||||||||||||||||||||||||||||||||||||||||||||||||||||||||||||||

20. The Whipping

THAT NIGHT AND AGAIN THE NEXT DAY HALLEY TRIED TO BRING up her Berry letter to her mother, but it was no use. "We're not talking about this now," Kate replied both times.

What she meant, Halley thought, was that she was *never* going to talk about it. It was like Daddy's death—something to pretend never happened.

On Tuesday it was bitter cold, but Kate decided the washing needed to be done while she was there to help. Though it would be good to have help for once, Halley had no heart for it. With little conversation, she followed her mother through the dreary business of doing the laundry in the kitchen.

Finally, the smells and the noise were too much for Pa Franklin. "I can't abide the stink of dirty clothes biling," he declared. "I'm going to see Billy Joe Eggar." The Eggars had a tight, warm house. "I'll likely eat with Billy Joe and his missus," he said as he headed out the door. Mrs. Eggar was known for setting a bountiful table.

Robbie tried to leave as soon as his grandfather was gone. "Mr. Calvin told me I could come today, didn't he, Halley?"

"Yes, but that was before," Halley answered, recalling how cold Mr. Calvin's face had become yesterday.

"You mean before Pa Franklin made the Calvins mad," Robbie asked.

Halley didn't answer, and finally Kate did. "You're staying home."

Robbie didn't give up. "See, it's not just me. If I take Golly with me, the Calvins will give him something to eat and let him stay in the lean-to next to the kitchen where it's warm."

"Old Man don't like Golly leaving the place," Ma Franklin said.

"Well, can I bring Golly inside just a little while so he can get warm?" The question was directed more to Halley than to Kate, but Halley ignored him.

Kate stirred the boiling pot of clothes with a stick, being careful not to splash it into the pot of beans simmering on the back of the stove. "You know the answer to that without asking," she finally said.

"Then I'll find him a place for a bed," said Robbie.

Halley was helping Kate rinse white clothes and dreading going out into the dogtrot to hang them.

"I don't know why we can't string up clotheslines in your room, Grandma. They'd dry faster, and we wouldn't freeze to death hanging things up."

Ma Franklin shook her head. "The old man won't allow it."

"Why not?" Halley asked, though she knew it was as hopeless as Robbie's pestering questions. "The room's empty except for the piano and the clothes hanging in the corner, and we wouldn't bother them."

Ma Franklin looked embarrassed. "You know Webb don't like nobody in that room."

"You'd think the room was filled with gold and jewels, the way he guards it!" said Halley.

Ma Franklin dropped her eyes.

At that moment they heard a noise in Ma and Pa Franklin's room. Halley threw open the door and saw Robbie standing next to the piano. "I was thinking I could play some while Pa Franklin was gone."

"Well, you can't," said Halley.

"I could pretend play," he said and sat down on the stool. Humming, he drummed his fingers on the piano lid.

Halley took his arm and led him back to the kitchen.

"I've been looking for a place to make Golly a bed," he announced. "I thought maybe the woodshed."

Ma Franklin shook her head. "Old Man won't like that. Dog hair'll git all over the wood and get brung in the house."

"Well, then how about the barn?"

Again Ma Franklin shook her head. "Webb runs him out ever time he catches him in the barn. Says he don't want a dog wallering on hay the cows and mules eat."

"The corn crib?"

"And git hair all over the corn we grind into meal? Lord no. Let the dog sleep under the house the same as he allus has."

"But it's cold under there, Grandma, and Golly's getting old."

"Let the dog manage as best he can," Kate said. "We got enough problems of our own, without borrowing from the beasts."

Halley finally took pity. "Make him a bed under the kitchen floor," she suggested. "Right under the stove would be a good place."

Robbie went back outside.

A short while later Halley was outside hanging laundry when she glimpsed Robbie coming from the barn with an armload of burlap bags. Golly trotted behind him. Robbie was wearing his Christmas boots, she noticed. Halley opened her mouth to remind him that they were only for wet weather, but then softened. Robbie looked up and she waved.

Pa Franklin was back before they'd rinsed the last batch of clothes. He came stomping in as though mad at the whole world.

"I thought you was eating with the Eggars," Ma Franklin said.

"I didn't get invited," he answered. "Billy Joe same as told me I wasn't welcome until I made things up with the Calvins."

"Oh, Webb! Him and Luke Calvin are the main ones that give to the church."

"Old Woman, I heared enough on that subject from Billy Joe hisself, without coming home to hear it from you!"

"I'm sorry," said Ma Franklin.

"And you ort to be," he said, pulling off his coat. "None of that business yesterday would've happened if'n you hadn't allowed your giddy headed granddaughter to go strollicking over to the Calvins." He turned to Kate. "And I blame you, too. The way you've commenced to carry on with Gravitt has set a bad example."

"You hold on a minute," Kate said. "I've not 'carried on,'

and I've not done anything sinful. And far as I can tell, Halley has done nothing wrong, either. Can't a person have some happiness on this earth without being doomed to hell forever?"

Halley looked at Kate in astonishment. Her mother's sudden boldness took her breath away. Apparently it knocked the wind out of Pa Franklin for a moment, too, because his answer did not come quite as instantly as usual.

"You better read your Bible and get right with the Lord," he sputtered. "Get ready for the Rapture!"

Kate blinked and took a deep breath. "Can't a body have a little joy in the here and now?"

"Find your joy in the Lord!" Pa Franklin threw himself down in his rocker and picked up his Bible from the table next to it.

For a time there was no sound except for the slosh of clothes Kate and Halley were wringing out, the ticking of the clock on the mantel, and the squeak of Ma Franklin's rocker. Then Halley heard a faint noise from the Franklin bedroom. Robbie must be in there again. Desperately she sloshed a pair of overalls in the tub to cover the noise while she tried to think how to send a warning. Before she could think of anything, there came a faint but unmistakable *thud*.

"Hey!" cried Pa Franklin, dropping his Bible and springing to the door. He threw it open. "Boy, what are you doing?" he bellowed.

"He just wanted to see his piano," Halley said.

"Did I ask you anything, girl? I'm talking to the boy. What are you doing?"

"Just . . . I was just . . ."

Ma Franklin got out of her chair and went to her husband's side. "It's not as cold coming through this way from the far room, Webb. And to tell the truth, it don't suck out the heat as bad as opening the door to the dogtrot hall."

Pa Franklin threw off the hand his wife had placed on his arm. "I got eyes, Woman. He ain't passing through. He's in here for something else." He turned back to Robbie. "So what are you doing in here?"

"I was going to pretend play my piano," he said, and he moved his hands across the lid of the piano, fingers striking imaginary keys.

Pa Franklin exploded. "I've told you and told you," he said, reaching for his belt. "But I guess *telling* you don't work. I reckon I'm going to have to *show* you I mean business."

"Don't," Halley said.

"This young'un broke the rules one time too many," Pa Franklin said, "and now he's going to get the punishment he deserves." He jerked his belt from around his waist and grabbed Robbie by the hand.

Kate stepped forward. "He's my child. I'll handle this."

"It's my house," answered Pa Franklin, "and my room he broke into. When I finish with him, he may remember the rules better."

"No," Kate said, stepping behind Robbie and putting both hands on his shoulders. "You're not whipping him this time. I'll handle this."

"We'll see about that," Pa Franklin replied, jerking Robbie free of Kate's hands. He headed for the door to the dogtrot. "We'll take care of this outside. The rest of you stay here." He threw open the door to a blast of cold air and headed outside with Robbie in tow. Kate was right behind them.

"You stay here, Grandma," Halley said and rushed after them.

"You are not doing this, Pa," Kate yelled. "I mean it." She caught them as they went down the steps to the yard and shoved Robbie into Halley's hands just as Golly came from under the house, barking.

"You can take your choice," said Pa Franklin. "I whip him or I whip you."

Kate drew herself up tall. "It'll have to be me, then."

"No!" Halley cried. This was worse than whipping Robbie. Far worse.

Robbie tore loose from Halley and threw himself at his grandfather. "I'll take the whipping. Don't hit my mama!" Golly began a wide circle around the four of them, growling deep in his throat.

From the porch came Ma Franklin's voice. The old lady stood there hugging a quilt around her. "Webb, you can't do this. What are you thinking?"

For a moment he seemed to hesitate, but then he said, "Old Woman, don't you try to tell me what to do. I'm still head of this house! You git back in the kitchen before you catch your death of pneumony fever." He kicked at Golly, who was still circling and growling. "Kate, step up here and take what's coming to you."

Kate squared her shoulders and stepped forward. "You need to think before you do this, Pa," she said in a quiet voice. "If you hit me, I'll be leaving here as soon as I can make arrangements."

Ma Franklin broke into tears. "Webb, can't you see? She's going to git married if you go through with this."

"I might get married," Kate answered. "Or I might board with somebody in Belton. Either way I won't be here long. And when I leave, it'll be the last money you'll ever get from me."

Again, Halley detected some hesitation in her grandfather. Then his face hardened. "Are you threatening me?"

"Take it how you will," Kate answered in an icy voice.

Pa Franklin raised the belt.

"Keep Robbie out of the way, Halley," Kate said.

Halley held her brother with both arms and hugged him so tightly that she could feel his heart beating against her chest.

"Don't, Webb," Ma Franklin begged once more. "Please don't do this. It's wrong, and bad things are going to come of it."

The first lick landed with a hard whack, and Goliath barked more loudly. As the blows continued to rain down, the fur raised on the dog's neck and the barking turned into fierce growling. Pa Franklin took time to land a kick on the dog's rump that sent Goliath sprawling against the corner of the steps. The dog yelped but was back up in a flash, circling again. Now his teeth were bared and his circle was growing smaller. The beating continued.

"Cry, Kate," Grandma Franklin said. "Cry and he'll stop."

But Kate refused to cry or to dodge. She stood with her arms folded and took the full force of every lick, staggering but never falling. Suddenly Golaith made a flying leap at Pa Franklin and knocked him to the ground. The belt went soaring through the air as the dog landed on his master's chest. The breath went out of Pa Franklin with a *whoosh*.

Ma Franklin screamed.

"Call him off, Robbie," cried Halley.

"Here, Golly," Robbie yelled. "Here!"

Golly obeyed reluctantly. Pa Franklin sat up and then stood slowly. Dazed and disbelieving, he looked toward his wife. She met his eyes for a long silent moment and then turned back toward the kitchen.

Kate retrieved the belt and handed it to him. "Do you want to whip me some more, Pa? I want you to be fully satisfied."

Pa Franklin took the belt without a word and laced it through his belt loops. Kate turned to Halley and Robbie.

"Let's go inside," she said. The three of them walked together while Pa Franklin followed alone.

The kitchen door stood open. The curtains at the window whipped in the draft that moved through the dim room. Pa Franklin slammed the outside door and the room became even dimmer. He looked around the room, blinking. "Ada?" he said.

Only then did Halley realize that her grandmother was not in the room.

"Ma?" said Kate.

Halley looked toward the bedroom door. It was still open. "Grandma?" she said, hurrying to the door. In the bedroom she saw her grandmother on her knees in front of the hearth. The old woman had pulled out four bricks and was digging out loose sand with her bare hands.

"What do you think you're doing, Old Lady?" asked Pa Franklin right behind Halley. "You're bothering what's mine!"

Ma Franklin did not answer. She pulled a metal box from the sand, opened the latch and threw open the lid to reveal money—green bills and silver coins. It was more money than Halley had ever seen.

Ma Franklin's gnarled fingers quickly counted out bills and held a fistful out to Halley. "The money he stole from you."

"No," said Pa Franklin, reaching for the bills too late. Halley had already stuffed them into her pocket.

"Half your money from the mill work and all the profit from selling your place," Ma Franklin said, handing a wad of bills to Kate.

"You can't do this," Pa Franklin said, snatching the money box from his wife's hands.

"I already done it," she answered. Tears were streaming down her cheeks. "I don't believe in you no more, Webb Franklin. You ain't the man I thought you was." Her voice was barely a croak, and her lips and hands were blue with cold.

Halley ran to help her grandmother to her feet. "You need to come get warm," she said.

Pa Franklin pointed to Halley and to Kate. "This is the thanks I get for taking you all in. You turn my neighbors and my church agin me, you take my dog away, and now you turn my own wife agin me!"

Ma Franklin turned. "Point that finger back at your own self, Webb Franklin. You the one done it. You the one that done it all."

In silence, Halley and Kate put Ma Franklin in her rocker and wrapped her in quilts. The old woman closed her eyes and sank down as though asleep, but the tears kept flowing. Nobody said anything. The terrible silence continued as Kate and Halley went back to the wash. Kate moved more slowly than before and when she turned, Halley saw a bloody streak on the sleeve of her dress. Halley gasped and reached out to touch it, but Kate shrugged off her hand.

It was a relief to escape that room to hang the last of the clothes on the line. It was misery to return to it. Though her grandmother was right, Halley felt an unwilling pity for Pa Franklin. The old man seemed as shrunken as his wife, and for once he did not seem to know what to say. Several times he cleared his throat as though to speak, but no words came.

At dinner they ate beans and cornbread in the same terrible silence. After the meal, Pa Franklin put on his coat and left the house. The cash box, Halley noticed, he left on the kitchen table.

Ma Franklin looked at it and then at the kitchen door. "Sometimes," she said slowly, "people find out too late what matters and what don't."

21. Called By Name

KATE WAS MOVING STIFFLY THURSDAY MORNING. SHE STILL wore the dress with the blood stain.

"You best put some salve on your arm and back," Ma Franklin said when she noticed it, "so them places will heal."

"I want 'em to take their time getting well," said Kate. "It'll keep me reminded what I've got to do."

When breakfast was almost ready and Halley went to the far room to get Robbie, she found Golly there, too. The dog was lying on a clean sheet with a pillow case wrapped around one leg.

"Robbie!" Halley said.

"Don't be mad," Robbie said. "Pa Franklin hurt Golly's leg yesterday and I'm doctoring it. I'll wash everything."

"You bet you will!" she answered, squatting to unwrap the dog's leg. As she expected, it wasn't injured seriously, but the blood and dirt spotted a number of places on both sheet and pillowcase. "In fact, you're going to scrub them right after breakfast, before it sets in," she said, letting the dog out. "And if Pa Franklin asks what you're doing, *you* can explain."

Robbie hung his head, but Halley refused to soften. "I'm sick and tired of trying to undo and cover up your mischief. If you hadn't been fooling with the piano yesterday, Pa Franklin wouldn't have got mad and whipped Mama. Ma Franklin wouldn't be mad at him, and Mama wouldn't be about to marry Bud Gravitt. It's all your fault."

"I'm sorry."

"You always are. Well, this time that's not good enough."

She was still angry at breakfast—too angry to eat. She nibbled at her biscuit while her gravy congealed on her plate. Nobody else was eating much either. Ma Franklin's food was untouched. The old woman huddled in her quilt wrapper, a far-away look in her eyes. Pa Franklin was the only one making much attempt at conversation.

He looked at Robbie just as Robbie put a biscuit in his pocket. He opened his mouth to speak, then seemed to think better of it. A moment later he said, "Boy, I noticed you left them new Christmas boots of yours out on the porch again."

This was Halley's cue to speak up and explain and defend as she always did. This time, however, she kept silent.

Pa Franklin drained his coffee cup and then looked from Kate to Halley. Neither offered to refill it, and so he finally got up to fetch the pot himself. "Boots cost money," he said when he sat back down. His eyes fell on the cash box still in the center of the table, and then his eyes skimmed over a letter propped against the box. He leaned closer and squinted at his wife's spidery handwriting. It was addressed to the eldest Franklin daughter.

"What you writing Eunice about?" he asked at last. "I hope you ain't about to do something foolish."

His wife did not look at him. "Nothing foolish," she said. "You can count on that."

Pa Franklin cleared his throat and changed the subject. "Temp Little told me yesterday when I went after Sukie that Trammell Pilcher's killing a hog tomorrow. Says he's looking for help. And you recollect he's generous in giving messes of fresh meat."

Kate looked toward her sewing machine where the dress pieces she had cut out yesterday were stacked. "I got a dress to make."

"I'm going to Carrie Gowder's to get more tea for Grandma," Halley said, realizing after she'd said it that this would only excuse her for today. "And I've got ironing to do tomorrow," she added.

"Mail my letter on your way to Carrie Gowder's house," Ma Franklin said to Halley.

"I can mail it for you," Pa Franklin offered.

"Thank you just the same," she answered. "I want Halley to do it. She don't break into other people's mail." She reached for the cash box, opened it and took out a quarter. "And give this to Carrie to put on her granddaughter's schooling. I'm allus proud to see somebody bettering themselves. I just wish my own granddaughter could do the same."

Pa Franklin's mouth opened to protest, but he stifled it and eased back into his chair.

As soon as breakfast dishes were over, Halley set Robbie to scrubbing the sheet and the pillowcase in a wash tub set next to the stove. Pa Franklin looked but asked nothing.

"I'm going to Carrie Gowder's," Halley said when it was time to leave. She half expected Pa Franklin to enforce the "no leaving the house" rule that he had pronounced on the way home from the Calvin's. But, again, he held his tongue.

Outside, Halley found Golly huddled on the porch next to Robbie's boots, licking his wound. "Robbie's working," she told him. "Why don't you get under the house before you freeze to death?"

In the pasture, she saw the cows. Maybe the cold weather would stop Sukie from escaping if the fence repairs didn't. Both cows were down near the pond, which appeared frozen over. Probably looking for water, she thought. Then she passed the earthen dam at the end of the pond and saw that below it the creek still flowed, though fringed with ice along the banks.

At the road she put her grandmother's letter in the mail-box and raised the flag. By this time Halley's cheeks and nose were stinging, and her feet numb. She ran to the cut off to the Gowder place. As she turned, she heard the sound of chopping off to the left. The Gowders needed lots of fuel. In addition to feeding fireplaces and stoves, they had big bricked-in outside ovens where they baked their pots. Judging from the stacks of wood around the edge of the yard, they must be getting ready to do some firing.

In front of Carrie Gowder's work shed, two colored men were loading a wagon with pots of all sizes. Between and around pots they placed burlap. Carrie came out of the shed with two large pots, and behind her came Opal with a churn. Trailing close behind was one of the dogs Halley remembered from her previous visit. He barked but kept his place behind Opal. The girl set down her load and laid a hand on the dog's head.

Carrie Gowder nodded at Halley in greeting and then turned back to the wagon. "Stack careful, Lige," she told the older of the two men. "These pots got to travel many a mile—all the way to Atlanta, if need be. But leave room for the dog bed. Major be giving out the alarm if anybody try to steal."

"And I don't git no pocket money?" the man asked.

Carrie shook her head emphatically. "Not this time, Lige. I done told you. You ain't spending Opal's school money." She turned to Opal. "Take Miss Ada's girl on to my living cabin and 'low her to warm herself. Fire be one thing we got plenty of."

As Opal and Halley headed toward the cabin, Carrie was inspecting the load of pots and suggesting improvements in placement and stacking. "Soon as this cold spell breaks, you gone to head out," she was saying.

"You're really and truly going to school?" Halley asked,

when she was inside the cabin and backed up to the fireplace.

A boy off to one side of the hearth laughed, showing a mouthful of white, even teeth. "Opal think she gone be a doctor or nurse."

Opal stared the boy down. Her face was fierce. "I *am* gone be a doctor or nurse someday. You'll see."

There was a long silence, and then Carrie came in.

"I want to go to school, but I don't know if I will," Halley said. "Times are bad."

"Times never gone be good," said Carrie Gowder. "Not lessen we makes 'em good by doing good things."

She was right, Halley thought. How come this old woman knew this, and her folks didn't?

"How Miss Ada doing?"

"Still ailing," Halley replied.

Carrie looked at the fruit jar Halley held. "Guess you've come after more tea."

Halley nodded. "And Grandma says to take this quarter toward Opal's schooling."

"Bless you," Carrie said and slid the coin into her apron pocket.

While Carrie went to her cellar to fetch the makings of the tea, Halley looked around the room. It was as clean as the Franklin house and perhaps better furnished. For sure, it was warmer. The bed in the corner looked as soft as a cloud. And, she suddenly realized, on the inside, Opal was more like her than anyone else she knew.

She thought about this on the way home. How unfair her life was—Opal would go to school and become a doctor or nurse, while Halley would probably end up working in the mill or maybe marrying and having eight or ten children. The future she was seeing was so bleak that it didn't seem worth living for.

She was still lost in these thoughts when she turned off the road by the Franklin mailbox. Moments later she saw Bud Gravitt's truck in front of the house. Then she saw Pa Franklin headed in her direction at a fast pace, his breathing making smoky puffs like a steam engine.

The last thing Halley wanted was another fussing out from him. Cutting off the road, she crawled through the barbed wire fence as if she wanted to look at the frozen pond.

"Girl!" he called. "Girl, you stop."

The word "girl" was like a slap, and she could suddenly endure it no longer. She swung around to face the old man. "I'm not answering to anybody calling me 'girl.' I've got a name."

Pa Franklin reached the fence and crawled through the wire. "All right, *Halley*. You satisfied?"

"Yes, sir," she said. She wanted to yell it. It was the first time he'd ever called her by name.

"You better be talking to your mama. Kate's about to make a big mistake."

Over her grandfather's shoulder Halley saw Golly running through the pasture, with Robbie right behind him. Then she realized that the dog had something red in his mouth. It looked like another version of the old game of "keep away." Suddenly she realized what the red thing was—one of Robbie's new rubber boots.

"You better be speaking up," Pa Franklin continued.

Halley shook her head. "Mama won't listen."

"Make 'er listen. You and your brother *think* I've been hard. Wait until you got a stepfather over you. Wait until you're in *his* house, eating at *his* table. Then you'd give a thousand dollars for the chance to be back here."

"I doubt that," Halley said.

Golly stopped for a moment and shook his head from side to side. Probably digging holes in the rubber with his teeth. Then as Robbie drew near, the dog took off again.

"Another thing," Pa Franklin said, "you need to say a few words to your grandmother. She taken a bunch of things wrong."

Halley took no pity. "You're the one who has to say something to her," Halley said.

"There's something in it for you, too," Pa Franklin continued on as if she had not spoken. "If your grandma gets back to herself and your ma sends Gravitt packing, I think you might be able to go to that there school when summer comes."

Halley was astonished. He must be desperate if he was willing to offer school as a bribe. But then he went further. "I might even see my way clear to help you get that headstone you wanted for Jim."

"I don't want your help," she answered. "If you hadn't emptied out my money box, I'd already have a stone on Daddy's grave. You're mean and stingy, and I don't want any help from you on anything."

"Listen to the pot calling the kettle black," said Pa Franklin. "Yeah, I guess I *am* stingy. But look at your own self—had nearly a hundred dollars hoarded away when your family was so hard up they didn't have two dimes to rub together. So who's stingier, you or me?"

The words took Halley's breath away. "I'm not like you," she said. "I'm *not*!"

"Is that right?" said Pa Franklin. "You kept your money in a make-believe book, and I kept mine in a tin box. How does that make you different?"

"Well, for one thing, I never stole money from somebody

else," said Halley. "I *worked* for it. And I wasn't saving it just for *me*. It was for me and my family."

"Stop!" Robbie yelled, and Halley saw that Golly had run out on the bridge of dirt that dammed the pond. He stopped halfway and shook his head just as Robbie got close enough to make a grab for the boot. Robbie only succeeded at knocking the boot out of the dog's mouth and sending it flying onto the ice. In a flash, Robbie was scooting down the embankment.

"No!" Halley screamed. "No! The ice isn't thick enough!"

Robbie didn't seem to hear. He was on the ice now and Halley could see it moving in waves. Then Golly was on the ice, walking so gingerly that Halley knew he must sense the danger. The dog grabbed the boot delicately, turned, and headed in a stiff legged walk for the bank. In several places a paw broke through before he reached the bank and climbed up it.

"Run that dog off," Halley screamed to her grandfather. "Don't let him back on the ice." To her brother, she said, "Lie down!" and for once Robbie obeyed, spreading himself face-down on the ice. Climbing down the bank, Halley swung out her arm to get him, knowing full well even as she did so that she could not reach him.

She needed a rope, a limb, something. Her coat! Jerking it off, she held it by one sleeve and flung it out to her brother. It didn't quite reach, so she tried again and again, getting her feet closer to the ice with each try.

Then her grandfather was beside her. "Crawl on your belly," he ordered. Halley saw a crack in the ice open and move like a snake toward her brother. She made one last desperate lunge for him and lost her balance. Suddenly she plunged through the ice and into the frigid water, going down, down to the depths of the pond. The world went black. She knew she was going to die.

HALLEY WOKE SLOWLY. VOICES surrounded her—her mother, her grandmother, Bud Gravitt, and Robbie. She blinked. She was wrapped in a quilt next to the stove in the kitchen. Her mother was crying.

"Oh, Bud, all she wanted was schooling, and I couldn't give her up."

"I was the same about you marrying," Halley wanted to say, but she didn't have the strength. She closed her eyes but could hear Robbie talking a mile a minute. "And Grandpa pulled me off the ice and then Halley fell in, trying to get me. And Grandpa jumped in and I thought they both would be dead . . ."

"Hush," said Ma Franklin.

"I'm going for a doctor," said Bud Gravitt.

With great effort, Halley opened her eyes again. "I'm okay," she said through chattering teeth. "Just tired and cold."

Kate knelt beside her and embraced her. "Another quilt. She needs more cover."

Halley wanted to close her eyes and sleep, but she realized there was one voice she had not heard. "Pa Franklin?" she said.

"Over here," Ma Franklin said, "wrapped in another quilt."

"I didn't know you could swim, Pa," said Kate.

"I didn't know it myself," came a muffled reply.

"He saved our life," said Robbie. "Grandpa's a hero."

"I reckon you're right," said Ma Franklin slowly. "I guess that does make Webb a hero."

"Thank you, Pa," said Kate. She broke into tears and Bud Gravitt put his arm around her.

"Mr. Gravitt is a hero, too," Robbie continued, "cause he helped get Grandpa and Halley in the house before they froze. Halley's a hero cause she tried to save me. And Golly would've been a hero if Grandpa hadn't run him off."

"Let it rest there," Pa Franklin said, "before you turn Sukie into a hero, too. Is that coffee about ready, Old Woman?"

"I'll get it for you right now, Webb."

From her place on the floor, Halley saw her grandmother's suddenly livelier walk and the peace that had come to her face. Before closing her eyes in sleep, Halley also saw Bud Gravitt pulling Robbie into an embrace with Kate, and she saw that this was, as Theodora said, what Kate had chosen for her life. For the first time Halley was willing to allow her mother that choice.

22. A New Beginning

IT WAS MID-MORNING ON THE LAST SATURDAY IN APRIL, AND the apple trees were in bloom. The Franklin house was scrubbed top to bottom, and most of the Owenby belongings were packed and piled in the dogtrot. The piano and the sewing machine were on the front porch, right up against the wall in case the overcast day brought rain. It was Kate's wedding day—the day all the Owenbys would move to the Gravitt house.

"Robbie, drag the sawhorses from the shed," Ma Franklin ordered in the brisk way she'd taken on since regaining her strength. "When the neighbors commence bringing in food for the wedding dinner, I want to have tables ready." She looked at the sky. "I believe the sun's going to come out after while."

Amazingly, Robbie obeyed his grandmother immediately instead of waiting to be told a second time or a third.

"That young'un's shaping up," said Ma Franklin approvingly.

"They's plenty or room for more improvement," said Pa Franklin.

Though it was only nine o'clock, Ma Franklin already had on her new ready-made dress, the first she'd ever owned. It was well-protected by an apron. Her bosom was a little higher, too. Halley had talked her into ordering a brassiere for the occasion.

"Old Man," she said, "I'll want a separate table for the lemonade and ice the Calvins are bringing. It's real neighborly for them to offer, and I want 'em to know we appreciate it."

"Hhumph!" said Pa Franklin, but he said no more. It was obvious that he was glad the differences with the Calvins had been patched up, and even gladder that his troubles with his wife were mended. Halley wondered if he'd actually told any of them he was sorry, but dared not ask.

Golly let out a "someone's here" bark, and Halley looked across the pasture to see Bootsie coming in a green dress that set off her red hair to perfection. She was carrying a Bible under one arm.

Kate came out of the house in the dress she had made after Christmas and saved for this day. "Is Gid going to make it?" she asked when Bootsie reached the yard.

Bootsie shrugged. "Depends on if he can catch a ride from camp." Bootsie laid her Bible on the porch and helped Robbie pull a sawhorse into place. She patted Golly on the head. "Mr. Franklin, you ought to allow this here dog to go back to Alpha Springs with Robbie."

"Allow it?" Pa Franklin said. "I'm a gonna *require* it. No dog can serve two masters, and that mutt made his choice several months back. He ain't worth no more than that dog, Buck. Golly ort to be a train dog, too. Hit'd be about the only thing he'd be good at."

"You mean I can *have* Golly?" cried Robbie, running to embrace his grandfather.

Pa Franklin stopped him with an outstretched hand. "You'll get my clothes dirty."

Bootsie picked up her Bible. "Kate, you and Halley and Robbie ready to go?"

"Go?" said Pa Franklin, turning his eyes on Kate. "It ain't time to go to the church yet."

Kate did not flinch, Halley noted, but met her father's gaze steadily. "We're going to walk. I figure to meet and talk to the preacher Bud is bringing to marry us."

"But Billy Joe Eggar was aiming to drive us there."

Bootsie smiled. "He can drive you and Ma. We won't start the wedding without you."

As soon as they were out of hearing, Halley said, "I can't believe Pa Franklin's letting us use his church for the wedding."

Bootsie giggled. "I don't think he's none too comfortable with it, but Kate made sure to ask him right in front of Billy Joe Eggar, and Billy Joe liked the idea."

Robbie tugged on Bootsie's arm. "If you're a preacher, how come *you* can't marry Mama and Mr. Gravitt?"

"Because she's not 'official' and ordained yet," said Kate. "She has to have people question her and say words over her and all that, but God will take care of that when the time comes."

Kate was sounding sure of herself on religious matters

these days, Halley thought. She had never been sure of anything before.

When the church came into sight, Halley had a surprise. There were three familiar vehicles out front—Bud Gravitt's truck, Theodora's rolling house, and Garnetta's car. Theodora was setting up her camera.

"Theo stayed special, to take pictures for us today," said Bootsie. "She's about to head back up North, and she's taking Opal Gowder to her school on the way."

"So Opal really is going to school," said Halley with envy. She felt her mother's eyes on her but did not return her gaze.

"Theo says she's through with her project on folks in mountain Georgia," Bootsie continued. "Well, I got news for her. She may be through with her *project*, but she ain't finished with us. She's part Georgia mountain now whether she likes it or not."

Theo heard this and laughed. "Dogged if I don't think y'all are right," she said in imitation mountain dialect.

Bud Gravitt stepped out of the church, smiling and holding up a bouquet of flowers. Annabel and Chub were with him.

Bud hurried to meet them, planted a kiss on Kate's forehead, and presented the flowers. He hugged Halley, too, before she could step out of his reach. "I'm glad you're going to be with us a little while before you go off to school at Berry," he said.

"Berry School!?" said Halley, turning to her mother.

Bud clapped his hand over his mouth. "You didn't tell her yet?"

Kate shook her head. "Haven't had a chance."

Halley threw her arms around her mother. "Thank you, Mama! Thank you! When?"

"How about June?"

"June," Halley whispered. "Yes. Oh, yes."

At that moment Bootsie's face lit up. "Gid!" she cried and ran to embrace her husband on the steps of the church. Garnetta came out with Dimple and Frank Earl, who were holding hands. Following them was a short, chubby man carrying a Bible.

"Folks, this is Preacher Clarence Clark," said Bud Gravitt by way of introduction.

"Let's go inside," the preacher said. "Ever'body set where you're comfortable."

Robbie sat with Garnetta, Bootsie, and Gid on the front row. Chub and Annabel led the way into one of the pews midway down the aisle and Halley followed, still in a daze from the news she'd just heard. Berry School! She was actually going to Berry.

Frank Earl and Dimple sat on the same pew with Halley.

"Old man Franklin would have a hissy fit if he knowed how many people here belonged to other churches besides Baptist," said Annabel.

Chub gave her a warning look. "Don't you stir up trouble."

"I already told you I ain't. I'm glad Pa and Kate are marrying. Now Baby Will can come home, and I don't have to do the cooking no more."

Chub winked at Halley. "And the rest of us don't have to die of innergestion."

Annabel gave him an elbow, and Chub bent over in mock agony.

Kate and Bud talked to the preacher at the altar until Ma and Pa Franklin arrived with Billy Joe Eggar and his wife.

Bud Gravitt turned to Bootsie. "Are we ready to begin?"

Bootsie nodded and walked to the piano. "I'm going to sing my favorite song," she said and began playing.

By and by, when the morning comes,
when the saints of God are gathered home,
We will sing the story how we've overcome,
For we will understand it better by and by.

"Ever'body join in and sing together," said Bootsie.

Halley sang with all her heart, and so did all the others. As they sang, the sun broke through the clouds and lit the inside of the sanctuary with golden light. Halley had never felt so good. She felt washed clean of all the bad things of the past year.

When the song ended, the preacher opened his Bible. "The morning *has* come," he said. "Bud and Kate have a new chance to make their lives all they want them to be, and so do all the rest of us."

Yes, Halley thought. That's exactly what it is—a new chance for Mama and Bud Gravitt and a new chance for me and Robbie, too.

It seemed to Halley that she floated through the wedding ceremony and the photographs that followed. She floated through the trip back to the Franklin house, too. When they got there, the neighbors had gathered and the tables were spread. Halley knew she would remember this scene forever as the time when a part of her life ended and another, better part began.

THE END

A Background Note

THE GREAT DEPRESSION HUNG ON LONGER IN THE MOUNTAINS of north Georgia than it did in most of the rest of the country. So, even though this story is set a little before my time, I didn't have to do much research. Many of the mountain communities where my folks lived did not get electricity until the late fifties and early sixties. Indoor plumbing came later than that. I grew up using kerosene lamps for light, wood-burning stoves for cooking, and wells for water. We had outdoor toilets and many of my relatives used mattresses stuffed with corn shucks. In my youngest childhood I walked with my grandmother to "meet the rolling store," and a few times I picked cotton. A sorry hand I was, too. Once my sister and I picked a small patch all by ourselves. It took us a full day, and together we had a little less than a hundred pounds.

Moonshining was not unknown in my family. Three of my great uncles were masters of the art. These were intelligent men, well educated for that time and place, but jobs were hard to come by, and they had families to provide for. They had many near brushes with the law, which made fine stories well after the fact. However, they eventually retired from the business after two of them spent time on a chain gang. Their tales about that experience made me and my four siblings vow to be law abiding!

My family attended fundamentalist Baptist churches, which preached a straight and narrow road to salvation. It always seemed a steep and joyless path to me. Whatever a body liked to do was almost bound to be sinful. Perhaps that is the reason backsliding was so common. As the years have passed I've come to a deeper appreciation for those who managed to stay on the path and live their faith. We had several preachers in the family, though none quite so hard-shelled as Pa Franklin in this story.

Even as a child I saw what a hard life women had. Most bore five to ten children, and those children were delivered by untrained midwives. My own mother married at fourteen and had me at fifteen with only her mother-in-law in attendance. The same grandmother also delivered the next two of my siblings. The third, a boy, weighed twelve pounds! Women had to scrub clothes by hand and press them with flatirons heated on a wood-burning stove. They canned goods from May through September and cooked three meals a day from scratch. Yet despite their hardships, women had little more than a child's say in the family.

Tufting bedspreads was one way mountain women could earn actual cash, but their husbands usually took the money. To make up for the earnings her husband took, one of my aunts used to "steal" a chicken every now and then to trade at the store for things she wanted–to her husband, she pretended hawks took the missing poultry.

One-room schoolhouses were common—I attended one for a few months when I was ten. Schooling beyond three or four years was considered a senseless luxury. As my mother said when I refused to drop out of school at age sixteen, "They won't pay you a bit more at the mill if you have a diploma in your hand." She *really* fussed when I decided to go to college. In fact, all five of Mama's children ended up finishing college, and she eventually saw the sense in it.

Franklin Roosevelt's CCC camps provided training and education—not to mention nutritious food and good clothing—to many a mountain boy. My mother's brother joined the CCC in 1936, and his stories of his adventures helped me with this book.

Theodora Langford is fictional, but she was inspired by several women photographers who took great risks to document events and people. Dorothea Lange, in particular, portrayed the face of Depression-era poverty in the photographs she made for the Farm Security Administration. I wanted Theodora to show Halley her Georgia mountain people and at the same time provide an example of what a woman could do.

Martha Berry, however, was a real person. Though she was born in 1865 to an affluent plantation family, she recognized even as a child the poverty and illiteracy all around her. As a young person she started her first school for the children of local farmers. In many cases, she had to convince parents that education was worth their children's time away from farm labor. In 1902 she began a boarding school for boys and in 1909 opened one for girls. From the start she planned for these young people to work while they learned so they could pay for most of their own education. Not content with serving local youngsters, she often traveled into the mountains with her father to recruit promising students. She was recruiting wealthy donors, too. By the time she established Berry College in 1926, she had set her sights on people like Henry Ford, who shared her vision for educating the children in mountain Georgia. Eventually, Ford paid for the building of a new girls' campus, using Gothic architecture and local stone.

Because Martha Berry died in 1942, I never knew her. But I was one of the Georgia mountain kids her schools educated. When I enrolled in 1957, many things had changed, but the school still had a work program that allowed students to earn most of their education costs and it still required uniforms.

During the Great Depression, the best place—often the only place—for a kid like Halley to get an education would have been Berry College.

No, I didn't need to do much research for this story. I just fictionalized my experiences and those of my family.

It's easy to cast a rosy glow over such bygone days, but on close examination I'd have to agree with Dolly Parton's song about her growing-up time: "A million dollars would not buy my memories of way back then, but for a million dollars I wouldn't live it all again."

— F. G.